b o o k s   t o   r e a d

TIMAS PUBLISHING

İstanbul 2012

timaspublishing.com

HAREM
Journey of Love
Aslı Sancar

TIMAS PUBLISHING | 2338
Fiction | 6

CHIEF EDITOR
Emine Eroğlu

EDITOR
Rifat Özçöllü

REDACTOR
Semra Borucu

COVER DESIGN
Ravza Kızıltuğ

FIRST EDITION
July 2010, Istanbul

FOURTH EDITION
November 2012, Istanbul

ISBN
978-605-114-262-3

TIMAS PUBLISHING
Alaykosku Caddesi, No:11, Cagaloglu, Istanbul, Turkiye
Phone: +90 (0212) 511 24 24 Fax: (0212) 512 40 00
P.K. 50 Sirkeci / Istanbul

timas.com.tr
info@timaspublishing.com
timas@timas.com.tr

Ministry of Culture and Tourism
Publisher Certificate: 12364

PRINT AND COVER
Sistem Matbaacılık
Yılanlı Ayazma Sok. No: 8
Davutpasa-Topkapı/Istanbul
Telefon: (0212) 482 11 01

HAREM
Journey of Love

Aslı Sancar

ASLI SANCAR

Born and raised in the USA, Aslı Sancar attended primary and secondary school in her hometown in Ohio. She later graduated from the Ohio State University with a major in English Literature. After working with the Federal Government for a year, she took courses on the MA level for one year during which time she served as a teaching assistant in the English Department at OSU.

After marrying her Turkish husband, Sancar's attention turned towards learning the Turkish language and culture and her new religion, Islam. She settled in Turkey in 1976 with her husband and two children. In 1978 their third child was born in Ankara. Having moved to Istanbul in 1984, Sancar began writing articles on women and the family for the newly published *Kadın ve Aile* magazine. In 1986 she wrote a small book about her journey to Islam, entitled *Islam'ın Işığına Uyanmak*.

During the early 1990's Sancar became interested in the subject of Ottoman women. Intrigued by the discrepancy between the Orientalist image of Ottoman women found in popular books and the Turkish heritage of Ottoman women, Sancar decided to research the subject for herself. She began her search in Istanbul with Turkish translations of European travelers' reports, but this quest eventually led her to original documents in a major university library in North America. There she was introduced to works of Western scholars who had come to Turkey and examined court records, palace records and other legal documents in regard to the rights and activities of Ottoman women. Based on her findings, Sancar eventually wrote a small book entitled, "*Osmanlı Toplumunda Kadın ve Aile*" which was published in 1999.

Wishing to share her findings on Ottoman women in English, Sancar wrote *Ottoman Women: Myth and Reality*. Her book earned the 2008 Benjamin Franklin Award in the politics/history category given by the IBPA, the largest association of independent book publishers in America. The book was also one of three finalists in the category of cover design. Sancar accepted the award at ceremonies held in Los Angeles, California, in May, 2008. She then spoke about Ottoman women on a book tour in various major American cities like New York City, Atlanta, Los Angeles and Washington D.C. In March, 2009, Sancar's book was published in Turkish under the title, *Osmanlı Kadını: Efsane ve Gerçek*. Sancar is also a professional translator and continues to follow works on Ottoman women.

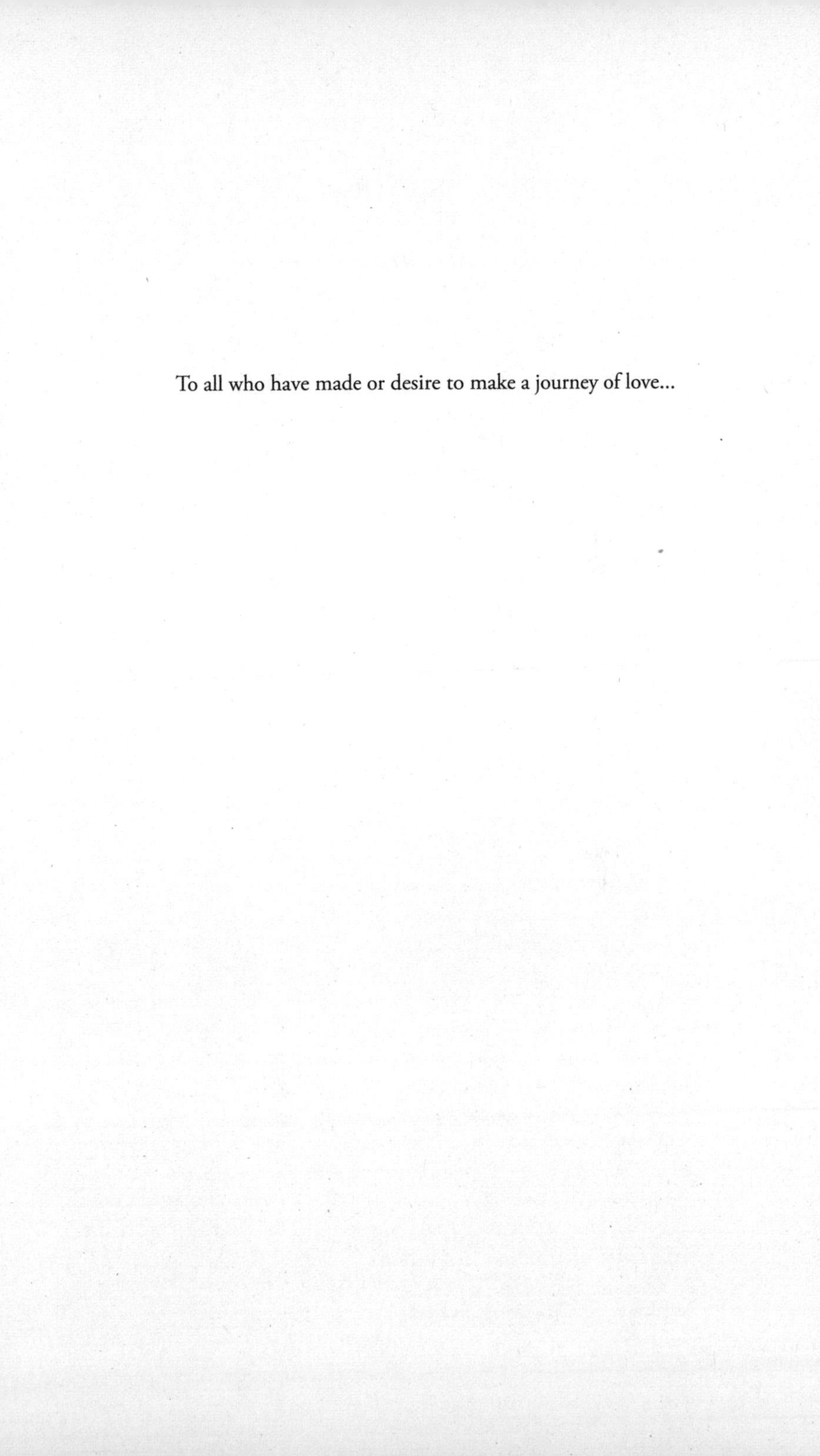

To all who have made or desire to make a journey of love...

I would like to express my sincere thanks to Afra Jalabi and my family for all their editing suggestions and help...

CHAPTER 1

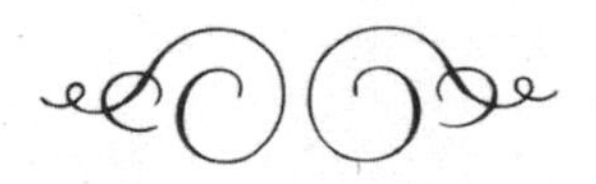

Spring, 1858

Southwest Circassia

The young Circassian girl's blue eyes were fixated on the graceful stallions as they raced back and forth in the broad green meadow near her village. Horses were the love of her life and the little seven year-old girl seized every opportunity to be near them.

"Sasa, come on," her older sister Janset called out. "We need to check our mare and see if she needs help. Her foal may be born any time."

With her eyes still riveted on the stallions, Sasa began trailing her sister in the direction of the village. Only the prospect of a new foal could have torn her away from the excitement of watching the spirited horses racing in the meadow.

The two girls headed straight towards the stable. Once inside Sasa ran to the mare's stall, but the horse's heavy belly told her that the foal had not yet been born. She softly stroked the filly's black mane and fed her some fodder from her hand. Sasa stayed in the stall for more than an hour until she was called into the house for dinner.

"Our mare's belly looks like it's about to burst," Sasa exclaimed. "I hope the foal will be born tonight."

"Don't worry, Sasa," her mother replied. "The foal will be born at just the right moment and not before."

Sasa was almost too excited to eat. She wanted to return to the stable, but her mother did not allow it. After finishing her chores, Sasa reluctantly got ready for bed. She prayed that the foal would be born during the night.

The next morning Sasa was up at the crack of dawn. Her mother was preparing breakfast as she entered the kitchen.

"Sasa, the foal was born late last night. You have to see it. The foal is black all over except for a large white star on its forehead."

"Sanneh*, can we call it 'Star'? Can we?" pleaded the little girl.

"Of course, Sasa," replied her mother. "I think that's a perfect name. If you like, you can go and see the foal while I finish preparing breakfast."

Sasa raced outside to see the new foal for herself. But due to the heavy morning fog, she could barely see the outline of the stable. Everything had taken on a dim and nebulous appearance in the thick fog. As she headed in the direction of the stable, Sasa heard a noise that sounded like the hoofbeats of a galloping horse. The sound drew closer and closer. Before she could understand what was happening, a horse and rider emerged from the fog and headed straight towards her. In a split second the skillful rider leaned sideways, scooped the little girl off the ground and threw her over his horse. Sasa was captured!

She cried out as the horse tore through the village, but no one seemed to notice her in the midst of the fog. Sasa was afraid of falling, so she clung to the horse's mane with all her might as they raced out of the village through the green meadow towards the mountains. Trees and bushes flew by in a blurred landscape. The horse galloped at full speed and kept up its lightning pace in spite of the mist that hung over the entire valley. It did not miss

---

* Circasian for "mother"

a step. Her home and village were soon left behind. When they suddenly approached a small stream, the skillful rider signaled the mount to jump over it. Horse and riders sailed through the air, clearing the water with ease. The horse settled into a more regular pace as the distance between them and the village increased. They finally slowed down at the bottom of a mountainous peak, and the three of them – the rider, the horse and the little girl - began an arduous trek up the mountain.

The horse was obviously accustomed to the rugged terrain. It stepped sure-footedly as they climbed up a narrow, rocky path. When the rider was certain they were not being followed, he stopped the horse, dismounted and put Sasa down on the ground. He looked into her frightened eyes and said:

"Don't be afraid, little sister. You're in safe hands."

The stranger took a silver water flask from the saddle and extended it to the girl. She made no reply, but took a long sip of water. The cool liquid had a calming effect as it flowed down her throat and chest.

The young man appeared to be in his early twenties. He was wearing a long, black fitted coat extending below his knees, fitted pants tucked into knee-high leather boots, and a white shirt with small buttons extending down from the high, round collar. His dress was topped off by a black, round fur hat. A dagger resting in a silver sheath hung at his waist.

Sasa had been warned many times by her mother and father about the danger of strange horsemen who stole little girls and sold them into slavery. She was never allowed to play by herself outside the village without an older relative or villager near by. But today the thick fog had concealed the lone rider and allowed him to take the girl by surprise.

The stranger took his cloak that was tied behind the saddle and wrapped it around the little girl before he put her back on the horse. The air had begun to chill as they climbed higher up the mountain path. He did not mount the horse, himself, but instead took hold of the reins and led the horse on foot. Briars and small twigs caught in Sasa's honey-blond hair as she rode along, but she was too numb to be concerned about them. It was as if the trauma of the capture had shut down her mental and emotional faculties and she was present only on the physical plane. She wasn't yet able to think about what would happen to her.

They continued traveling all day long in the heavily wooded terrain until just before dusk when they passed through a narrow gap between two snow-covered mountain peaks. Climbing even higher, they entered a dense thicket of trees. Much to Sasa's surprise, a solitary, make-shift cabin stood in the middle of the thicket. The rider halted the horse and helped Sasa dismount. Then he motioned for her to go inside. While he led the horse to a small shelter nearby, Sasa slowly advanced towards the cabin. Not knowing what to expect inside, the little girl's heart was beating wildly as she slowly undid the latch. The door swung open and Sasa looked inside. All she could make out in the dark, one-room structure was a crudely-built fireplace and two sleeping pallets on the floor. A few bags of provisions hung on the walls. Sasa saw no immediate threat, so she ventured in.

A few minutes later the young man came in and lit a small gas lantern. The smoke-stained glass chimney cast a dim, uneven light in the stark room. Sasa huddled down on one of the pallets on the floor. She was shivering from the cold. It was a relief for her to see the young man starting a fire in the fireplace. Putting some potatoes and carrots into an iron pot of water, the stranger began making a stew. The warmth from the fire made Sasa drowsy, and only the knawing in her stomach kept her awake. Once the stew was ready, Sasa ate her share and then immediately drifted off to sleep.

Towards dawn Sasa suddenly woke up. She was in a heavy sweat, although the coals in the fireplace had long since died out. The thunder of hoof beats and the sound of her own screams lingered in her ears as she passed through a twilight zone between nightmare and wakefulness. As she became fully conscious, these sounds gave way to the voice of the stranger:

"Get up, get up, little sister. We have to start off shortly."

Sasa sat up with a start. When she remembered the events that had brought her to this cabin in the woods, the heaviness in her chest returned.

Timidly she asked, "Where are we going?"

"We have a long journey down the mountain to catch the ship sailing for Istanbul," replied the stranger.

"Ship? Istanbul?" echoed Sasa. Now she understood what was in store for her.

Kidnapped young girls and boys with attractive features were sold to slave dealers. They brought handsome prices. The dealers sold them, in turn, for substantial sums of money to Ottoman palace officials in Istanbul or members of the Ottoman ruling elite.

Hearing these words, Sasa became even more frightened. She didn't want to leave her homeland; it would end any hope of ever seeing her family again…

The stranger put some cold stew and hard bread in front of Sasa. Then he prepared some provisions for the day's journey. Seeing the fear in Sasa's eyes, he said to her:

"Don't be frightened, little sister. Many have made this journey before you. Your life will be better than you could ever dream of."

The little girl sipped her stew. She didn't fully understand what the stranger meant, but she felt a little comforted by the tone of his voice.

The young man was eager to begin the journey. As soon as she finished eating, he got up and went outside to ready his horse. He motioned to Sasa to follow him.

Again the stranger mounted Sasa on the horse. He walked at her side with the horse reins in one hand and a long, slender-barreled rifle in the other. As they headed down the mountain, the early morning air was cool and crisp. Little rivulets of water rushed down the side of the mountain, flowing faster than they could walk. The forest was alive with the sound of birds chirping above their heads as they descended down the trail. Sasa saw three deer break into flight as they passed close by them. As the morning wore on, rays of bright sunshine burst through empty spaces between the trees and warmed them. Even a few wild flowers had begun to bloom in the narrow plateaus they occasionally crossed. Signs heralding both an end and a new beginning were present everywhere.

The stranger and the little girl had descended the mountain and were following a trail that would take them to the Black Sea in several hours. Having already reached its zenith, the sun was beginning to move towards the West. The weather was milder now and the meadows were full of spring flowers. The stranger pointed to a large tree near the bank of a stream and then led Sasa and the horse there. They refreshed themselves by washing their faces and arms in the cool water. Then after they sat down to rest a little, the stranger took a saddle bag of provisions and handed some cheese, bread and dried fruit to Sasa. While she ate, he led the horse to the river to quench its thirst. Sasa did not say a word nor did she even dare to think of escape. She knew she was no match for the daring and experienced stranger.

After a twenty minute rest, they moved on. They had to reach the slave trader's boat that sailed for Istanbul on the same day every month. The boat picked up slave captives from the Caucasus, sold them to brokers in Istanbul and then brought trading goods back to the Caucasus to sell.

When they reached the coast, there were already many young people aboard the ship, which was anchored near a small settlement close to the Black Sea. Some of the children were from slave families and had been sold to the slave dealer by their owners. Others had been captured against their will like Sasa. Still others from poor families had volunteered to be sold into slavery in order to ensure a better future for themselves. It was widely known that slavery in the Ottoman Empire could be a ladder for upper mobility in society.

The slave trader was standing on the shore talking with some men with whom he had just closed a deal. The stranger walked over to the slave dealer. It was obvious that they knew each other well. After twenty minutes of heated bargaining, the men came to an agreement. The stranger was paid, and Sasa was sent to join a small group of slaves who would be taken to the large ship in a long narrow rowboat.

Sasa boarded the ship with a heavy heart. She knew she was probably seeing her Circassian homeland for the last time. She also knew that she would most likely never see her family again.

On the deck the doors to two large freight holds were open. Males were being sent down into one hold, and females into the other. The little girl had difficulty adjusting her eyes from the daylight outside to the dimness in the hold as she stepped down the rungs of the ladder. Also, the heaviness of the air in the crowded hold made her catch her breath. Sasa carefully scanned the faces as the pupils of her eyes adjusted to the dim atmosphere. There must have been at least fifty young women and girls in the cramped hold. The trap door to the hold was being closed. As it shut out the last rays of the fading sun, it also extinguished the last glimmer of hope in the little girl's heart.

The swaying of the boat, the atmosphere dense with the breath of so many people in an enclosed space, and the weariness from the long day's march all collaborated to bring immediate sleep to Sasa and most of the others in the hold. The boat had caught a good wind and was sailing swiftly towards Istanbul, away from the Circassian homeland to a completely new and unknown realm.

Again, the night passed in nightmares for Sasa: villagers shouting, horses whinnying, cattle braying, dogs barking – she could hear them all, but she could see nothing except the murky fog. Her mother called out to her, but then her voice faded away and was absorbed into the fog. Everything was swallowed by the fog. The fog became an entity – a dangerous, sinister entity – that swallowed the whole village. It was just about to swallow Sasa, too, when she was awakened by the opening of the door to the hold.

She sat up startled by the noise. The first signs of daylight appeared in the sky above the open hatch. Other girls started to stir around her. Sasa was happy to realize that the fog was only a part of her nightmare. She even felt safety in the large number of other girls around her in the hold of the ship; she was definitely not alone. A few minutes later one of the crew members started to hand down large baskets of bread and cheese and round earthen jugs of water. The smell of the bread and cheese reminded the girl of how hungry she was. The food was just enough to stave off everyone's hunger for a while.

The girls began talking with one another, but in hushed voices, as if there was a rule forbidding them to speak loudly on the ship. Sasa listened carefully to the others around her. She had recently heard her mother and her aunt talking about life in Ottoman harems. They had both agreed that slavery could lead to a bright future for young girls and boys, so Sasa was not surprised to hear a young teenage girl speak enthusiastically about it:

"Last summer a *saraylı** returned to visit our village. Her family members were slaves in our village and the girl was sold by her master when she was ten years old. She was bought by the royal palace and taken there to live. Everyone treated her very kindly. In fact, she felt like they were her family. She received beautiful gifts of jewelry and clothing on special occasions and she was even taught to play the *kemençe***. She told wonderful stories about events and people in the palace, and she said that living there was the best thing that ever happened to her."

---

* A female slave from the royal palace or *saray*.

** A small violin with three strings played like a cello.

"Why did she leave, then?" another young girl asked.

"She said she wanted to have her own family and mansion, and she did. The Sultan arranged a marriage for her with one of his pashas* and gave her a house and furnishings. After her husband died, she came to visit the village with two of her children and she brought many gifts with her."

Another teenage girl told about two girls in her village volunteering to be sold. Their parents approved because the family was very poor and they believed the girls would have a better future in Istanbul. But there were also stories of sorrow: kidnappings, boats capsizing in the rough waters of the Black Sea before they reached Istanbul, captives dying on board from contagious diseases. It appeared that almost every girl in the hold had something to say about the road to slavery in the Ottoman Empire.

Sasa listened intently to these stories all day long. Some of them sounded almost too good to be true. Was it really that easy to marry a prince or a pasha? Did all the Circassian girls become rich? She didn't think so. Even if these stories were true, she would rather be back in her village with her parents and brothers and sisters, playing under the open skies and taking care of Star. She missed her family terribly.

It was as if the iron hand of fate had seized Sasa from the village, robbing her of her Circassian homeland and family. Fate had stripped her of everything she held dear. Now, cramped into the ship's dim hold, Sasa was being rocked in life's womb. Whether she wanted it or not, the little girl was soon to be born into a new life.

The sailing ship was almost enveloped in darkness again. A member of the crew handed down biscuits, dried fruit and water for the girls. After everyone ate their share, they again succumbed to sleep. The boat glided through the dark waters of the Black Sea, following along the coast line in deep waters. Although the

---

* A general.

stars were out, the new moon was just a sliver in the nighttime sky. It gave off very little light. This presented no problem to the ship's captain, however, because he had traveled these waters many times. This route was as familiar to him as the back of his hand.

The night passed fretfully again for the little girl. This time she dreamed she was walking away from her village down a narrow dirt path. She felt as if she had forgotten something, but she couldn't remember what. As she continued on her way, she suddenly remembered what it was: the small silver locket her grandmother had given her. The locket contained a prayer that her grandmother said would protect her from evil, so she had to go back and get it.

She was returning to the village when a frog jumped in front of her. The frog was wearing the locket around its neck. She tried to catch it, but the frog leaped into a nearby stream. The locket fell from the frog's neck to the bottom of the stream and was swallowed by a fish. The little girl jumped into the water and was about to catch the fish, when the fish jumped out of the water and started to hop away. She scurried out of the stream and ran after the fish. Just as she was about to catch it, a bear came out of the forest and grabbed the fish. She wrestled with the bear to get the fish, but it was too strong for her. The bear growled fiercely and barred its sharp teeth. It was about to sink its teeth into her throat when Sasa suddenly woke up.

Her heart was pounding. The bear's growl was still ringing in her ears. Realizing it was just a nightmare, she looked around at all the sleeping girls, touched the locket around her neck and again felt safe and secure in the cramped hold. The rocking motion of the boat soon made her drift off to sleep again.

The opening of the door to the hold woke Sasa just as it had the day before. She stood up and stretched her legs as best she could. After eating the provisions sent down to them, the girls were allowed to go up on deck. The weather was overcast with the sun hidden behind the clouds. The girls had been on deck no more than twenty minutes when a strong wind began to blow and the waters became choppy. When the first drops of rain began to fall, one of the captain's assistants told the girls to go back down into the hold.

Shortly the boat began to rock back and forth in the water. Rain dredged the boat of helpless captives. Thunder reverberated in the dark skies and lightning crackled everywhere. Sasa soon felt nauseous from the constant rolling of the boat. She looked around and saw that the faces of almost all the girls had paled. Some of the girls began to cry and moan. Others ran to the latrine buckets to vomit. The wind seemed to be playing with the boat, testing it to see how much heaving it could take. The wooden boat, on the other hand, was creaking and groaning under the assault, in immediate danger of breaking in two.

Everyone was terrified, including Sasa. She had never experienced anything like this. It seemed as if the boat would capsize at any moment. Sensing that the boat and all those in it were totally at the mercy of God, Sasa prayed as she never had before. She promised she would have no more complaints if only God would spare her life.

The storm continued throughout the night, pushing the endurance level of the girls to new heights. At the point where Sasa felt she could take it no more, the storm began to subside. The wind died down, the rain dwindled and the heaving of the boat stopped. Exhausted by the stress of the storm, the girls all fell asleep at dawn.

The next day when they woke up, the girls were again allowed to go up on deck. The sun was shining brightly and the sea was calm. A soft, warm breeze caressed the cheeks of the girls as they looked out over the horizon, as if to apologize for the roughness of the storm.

The next three days passed uneventfully. Sasa did not even have any more nightmares. But on the seventh day of the journey there was a special buzz of excitement in the air. The girls had been told they would arrive in Istanbul by evening. On the one hand, this news pleased Sasa, because she was eager to get out of the boat's cramped freight hold and step on solid ground again. But, on the other hand, she had no idea of what was going to happen to her. The uncertainty made her stomach hurt. She wished with all her heart that she was back in her Circassian homeland.

The sailboat again picked up a strong wind and glided effortlessly over the sea. The ship sailed so swiftly that it arrived at the mouth of the Bosphorus Straits earlier than the captain had anticipated, so he threw down anchor there and waited several hours for the cover of darkness to come. Due to pressure from the British and French, the Ottoman authorities had outlawed the slave trade from Africa, but they still permitted slaves to be brought from the Caucasus and Georgia. However, in order to avoid any interference from the British, the captain waited for night to fall before he entered the straits.

When the boat finally docked, the slaves were picked up by brokers and taken to houses in the districts of Galata and Beyoglu. Sasa was taken by carriage, along with about twenty other young girls, to a large house in Beyoglu. They entered the enclosed garden through a large wooden door. Then the group climbed up a long marble staircase that led to a porch with two separate entrances. The broker, the drivers and the other male servants entered the *selamlık** door. The broker's wife opened the door to the *harem*** and ushered the girls inside. They were taken into a spacious anteroom that was furnished with Persian carpets and European furniture. The broker's wife, Madame Theodora, was a stout, middle-aged woman. She wore a long, European-cut

* Quarters in the house reserved for male adults, male servants and male visitors.

** Quarters reserved for female members of the family, female servants and female guests. The master of the house also had a room(s) there.

orange and purple striped dress that didn't become her bright red hair. The woman had a cold look on her face and her behavior was all business. Sasa didn't trust her and instinctively kept her distance from the broker's wife.

Three servant girls brought in several large round metal trays. They spread cloth covers on the floor and then set the trays on top. Madame Theodora motioned for the girls to sit around the trays. Soup, bread, rice and several vegetable dishes were brought in for them to eat. The girls ate in silence. As soon as the meal had finished, the trays were removed and beds were made up on the floor for the girls to sleep on. Exhausted by their journey, everyone shortly sank into deep sleep. A gas lamp was left burning and two of the female house servants sat in the room on guard throughout the night.

Sasa fell into a deep and restful sleep. The events of the past several days had physically taken their toll on the little girl, and now her body was taking this opportunity to renew and regenerate its vital forces. Just before dawn she began dreaming about her village again. It was night time and a strong wind was howling through the village. Sasa was in the stable with Star. She was stroking the young colt's forehead.

"Don't worry, my beautiful Star, I won't allow anyone to hurt you," she said in a soothing tone of voice.

The foal looked up at the little girl as if it understood exactly what she said. Sasa put her arms around Star and gradually the two of them fell asleep. After a little while she woke up, but the foal was gone. Sasa ran from one corner of the stable to another.

"Star! Star! Where are you? Where have you gone?" she cried out with panic in her voice.

"Please, Star, let me know where you are!" she pleaded.

The stable door was open and she heard a faint whinnying sound outside. She bolted to the door and ran out into the darkness. An indistinct figure was bent over Star, who was tied to the cutting block where wood logs were split. The figure had a hatchet in its hand. As the figure raised the hatchet to strike the helpless foal, Sasa leapt into the air and tackled the figure. With the impact of the tackle, the hatchet struck the stranger instead of the colt, and the mysterious figure fell to the ground. Sasa grabbed the hatchet and cut the rope binding the foal to the cutting block. Then she looked at the figure lying lifeless on the ground. It was Madame Theodora!

Sasa suddenly woke up, opened her eyes and looked around the room. Most of the other girls had begun to wake up, as well. The door opened and Madame Theodora entered the room. Sasa was even more wary of the slave broker's wife now. The woman began talking with the two female servants who had spent the night on guard. Sasa overheard her ask the servants:

"Did any of the girls snore loudly?"

"No, Madame," one of them replied, "don't worry, we heard no such noise last night."

If a new slave girl snored at night, the purchaser might send her back to the broker or pay considerably less than the price agreed upon. Madame Theodora had a look of relief on her face.

The slave girls on duty left and two more servants came in to pick up the beds. They were carried into the next room and stored in large built-in cupboards. Meanwhile, a mid-wife came in to examine the girls for any physical defects and to control their virginity. They were examined individually behind a silk screen. Non-virgin girls sold for only half the price of virgins. Madame Theodora assured the girls there was nothing to be concerned about; all slave girls had to be examined before they were sold. In spite of this, however, the girls were very shy and embarrassed. Fortunately the mid-wife had a motherly demeanor and treated the girls gently. Madame Theodora was pleased to learn that the girls were all virgins.

As soon as the examinations were over, the trays were set up again for breakfast. Large baskets of bread and buns were brought in, and goat's milk cheese, hard-boiled eggs, black olives, rose jam and hot tea were placed on the trays. Sasa noticed the beautifully embroidered linen napkins the girls were given to put in their laps at breakfast.

After the girls had taken their fill and washed their hands, they were all led into a room midway between the *selamlık* and the harem. When the door opened from the male quarters, Sasa was amazed to see a distinguished-looking black man walk through the door. She had never seen a black person before; in fact, she didn't even know black-skinned people existed.

The man, Rauf Efendi, was the Chief Agah of the House of Felicity, or the imperial harem. He was the highest ranking black eunuch in the Ottoman administration. His position was very prestigious and carried high responsibility. This was obvious by the way he dressed. He wore a rich, dark suit of clothing and a red fez on his head. The collar of his long suit coat was made of black velvet; inside the coat he wore an immaculate white shirt and a red and grey colored tie. His ring made from a huge red ruby set in gold sparkled on his finger.

Rauf Efendi was there to buy some girls for the royal palace. While the slave broker was extolling the merits of girls he was seeing for only the second time, the Agah carefully looked at each of them with a discerning eye. He had bought many slave girls before, and he knew well the high standards of the palace. He chose only four girls. And one of them was Sasa…

After the business transaction was completed, the girls were taken outside where the royal carriage was waiting. The beautiful horses attracted Sasa's attention and she wondered what had happened to Star. Rauf Efendi sat next to the driver and the four girls rode inside the carriage. Two colorfully dressed guards stood on the sides of the carriage near the front. Sasa could not see out because there were tightly closed curtains at the windows. The interior of the carriage was upholstered in rich red velvet and the ceiling was gilded in intricate designs. The little girl was curious about the outside world, but she didn't dare open the curtain. The girls just stared at each other silently, with no idea of what would happen to them next.

Chapter 2

Summer, 1858

Beylerbeyi, Istanbul

On the other side of the Bosphorus shore in Beylerbeyi, Jamila Hanım was adjusting her veil in front of a large oval mirror in the harem entrance to her *yalı*.* The mirror was almost the only sign of Western influence in the mansion's furnishings. Jamila and her husband Kamil Bey were both very much tied to Turkish customs and traditions. Even though Kamil had studied medicine in France, he was still conservative in his outlook on life. Their large two-storey wooden mansion had been built by Kamil's father according to traditional Turkish architecture and furnished in Turkish décor. The house had two separate entrances, one for men and the other for women. Male guests were hosted in the large reception room on the second floor in the male quarters, and male slaves had their sleeping quarters on the first floor.

The main reception room in the harem was huge with a large, three-tiered marble fountain in the middle. The water made a soothing sound as it flowed from one tier to another. The room was very light with a number of long windows facing the straits. Above these there were smaller stained-glass windows that allowed in even more light. The room was furnished mainly by low, built-in

---

* Turkish mansion located on the sea shore.

Ottoman sofas which were covered in costly, eggshell white silk material embroidered in silver thread. There were several large Turkish carpets on top of Egyptian reed matting that covered the wooden floors. The built-in wooden cabinets and the ceiling were painted in pastel floral patterns with gilding that further gave an air of lightness to the room. The only other furnishings were small octagonal tables inlaid with ivory and large brass braziers used for heating in cold weather. Framed works of calligraphy, most of them verses from the Quran, adorned the walls. Although the room was sparsely furnished, each item from the small rose-water ewer to the large marble fountain was, in itself, a work of art, for everything was skillfully and profusely embellished with intricate designs.

Jamila was about to depart with two of her *kalfas** to visit Rabia Hanım, a childhood friend of hers living in Kanlıca, also located on the Bosphorus Straits. It was not socially acceptable for Ottoman women -except elderly ones- to go out without companions. Plus the two senior *cariyes*** were skillful seamstresses, and today many of Rabia's friends and acquaintances were gathering in her mansion in Kanlıca to prepare a trousseau for a young neighborhood orphan girl soon to be married. The driver brought the carriage around to the front of the house, and Jamila and her two slave women settled in.

As the carriage began its slow journey along the narrow, winding road running along the coast, Jamila's thoughts drifted back in time to when she was helping to prepare her own trousseau. Although her mother had begun preparing it from the time she was born, as did most Ottoman mothers, there were still many last-minute details to be completed when Kamil had asked her father for her hand in marriage.

---

* Senior-ranking servants.

** Female slaves, pronounced "jariyah."

Jamila had had offers of marriage from the time she was fifteen years-old. Due to her father being a well-respected religious scholar, their family wealth and the young girl's beauty, Jamila had been a frequently sought after bridal candidate. But Jamila was determined not to marry until her heart told her it was the right thing to do. None of the prospective grooms met her expectations until Kamil.

When Jamila was eighteen years old, Makbule Hanım, a distant relative, brought a picture of Kamil. He had just returned from France after finishing his medical degree and had been assigned to the imperial palace as a doctor to young male students at the palace school. Knowing Jamila's high standards and expectations, Makbule *Hanım** had thought it wise to consult the girl before she encouraged Kamil's mother to come and see the prospective bridal candidate.

Jamila looked at the photograph carefully. Kamil was handsome and intelligent looking, and his appearance impressed the young girl. Jamila believed she saw both gentleness and strength in Kamil's dark eyes, qualities she was looking for in a husband. After getting the young girl's approval, Makbule Hanım informed Kamil's mother that an appointment had been arranged for her to meet Jamila and her mother in their home in Kanlıca.

In Ottoman society it was custom for marriages to be arranged by a third party, who might be a relative, a match-maker or just an acquaintance. Unless they knew each other as children, it was probable that the bride and groom would not see each other before they married. However, the consent of the bride was required.

On the morning of the appointment Jamila got up early and carefully chose what she would wear that day: an emerald green caftan fitted at the waist over aqua-blue silk pants and a short black velvet vest embroidered with gold thread in a paisley design. A small green cap, black velvet slippers adorned with sequins and an emerald pendant her grandmother had given her completed her

* A term of adress to men's wife.

outfit. She had her childhood *dadı,** Gulshah, braid small jewels into her long, thick black hair. Gulshah Dadı was a middle-aged Circassian woman whose beauty had only recently begun to fade. She had taken care of Jamila since she was an infant and was like a second mother to the girl. She knew this was an important day by the unusual gleam in Jamila's dark eyes.

When Makbule Hanım and Kamil's mother, Seniha Hanım, came to call, they were met by a servant and escorted into a large reception room in the harem where Jamila's mother, Safiye Hanım, was expecting them. As was custom, after introductions and a short exchange of pleasantries, Jamila brought in three demitasses of Turkish coffee on a silver tray. Although girls were supposed to keep their eyes lowered, Jamila was careful to discreetly get a good look at Kamil's mother. She knew that mothers have a great influence on the development of a child's character, so Jamila wanted to see what kind of person the woman was. Also, it was custom in Ottoman society for widowed women to live with their sons. Although Seniha Hanım was not a widow, there was always a possibility that she could be in the future. Even if they didn't live together, Jamila knew that mothers-in-law had great authority in the family.

Seniha Hanım did the same. She carefully followed every movement Jamila made with a discerning eye, because her son would not have an opportunity to see the bridal candidate up this close until after he married her. So Seniha Hanım's impressions of Jamila were of paramount importance. She had talked in great detail with Makbule Hanım about Jamila's family background and the girl's childhood and character. Her husband had also made serious inquiries about Jamila's father and even their ancestors. The results of all these inquiries were encouraging, but Jamila's physical appearance, personality and demeanor were also very important. She had to be Kamil's *denk* or equal. Custom didn't allow much

---

* Nursemaid.

time for observation. As soon as the coffee cups were emptied, Jamila gathered them together on the tray and excused herself from the room. After a few minutes more of polite conversation, the two women guests asked for permission to leave and Safiye Hanım showed them out.

As soon as she closed the door, Safiye Hanım asked a servant to call Jamila to the sitting room. When Jamila came in, she noticed that her daughter's face was a little flushed.

"Well, Jamila, what do you think?" asked her mother.

"*Anneciğim,** first I want to hear what you think," replied Jamila.

Safiye Hanım proceeded cautiously. She didn't want to encourage her daughter too much before they heard from Kamil's family.

"I tried to understand what kind of mother she would be for you, Jamila. Would she be kind and considerate of you? Would she be supportive of you? Would she be fair? These are the questions that ran through my mind while we were talking. What were you thinking, Jamila?"

"Anneciğim, I asked myself similar questions," Jamila replied.

Safiye Hanım continued, "I understand from Makbule that the family's social standing and life-style are very compatible with ours. They, too, are strongly traditional, on the one hand, but obviously they are open to change as well since they sent their only son to be educated in France. But the truth is, my dear Jamila, it is very difficult to know someone fully if they don't want to be known. Polite inquiry is not enough. If they ask for your hand, I'm going to make the *istihare*** prayer and see what my dreams reveal before we give them an answer. And what was your general impression, my dear?"

"My first impression was positive, but, of course, it's too soon to tell," replied Jamila. She, too, gave a guarded answer, because

---

* My dear mother.

** Divination by dreams.

her mind told her not to get her hopes up before she knew Kamil's intentions. Her heart, however, had already taken wing.

A response was not long in coming. Kamil's father and uncles were going to ask for Jamila's hand in marriage from her father, Hikmet Efendi. Jamila's father immediately began inquiries regarding Kamil's family. He sought out mutual acquaintances who had known both families for a long time. He not only investigated the career path of Kamil's father, but he also contacted the Ottoman ambassador in Paris who was sure to know of Kamil's activities in France.

Meanwhile, Safiye Hanım made a special prayer with the intention of learning whether or not this marriage would be auspicious. Then she went to sleep. In her dream she saw her deceased god-mother, Hayriye Ana, who had been a very spiritual and saintly woman. Anytime Safiye Hanım saw Hayriye Ana in her dream, she knew it was reliable. She and her god-mother were walking up a long flight of stairs. When they finally got to the top, which was the seventh floor, there was a room with an open door in front of them. The two women looked inside. Jamila was sitting in the middle of the room, but she was just a child six or seven years-old. She was playing with a doll and didn't look up. Turning to her god-mother, Safiye Hanım asked:

"What's Jamila doing here?"

"Oh, you don't know it yet," replied Hayriye Ana, "but Jamila is going to climb very high in this life."

Then Safiye Hanım woke up. She could still feel the presence of her god-mother. She could even smell the essence of rose oil that Hayriye Ana always used. Safiye Hanım gave a sigh of relief. She interpreted the dream as a positive sign for Jamila's marrying Kamil.

That evening when Jamila's father returned home, Safiye Hanım told him about her dream.

"Hikmet Efendi, I made the *istihare* prayer today, and I saw a dream. God willing, it is a good omen," said Jamila's mother.

"What did you see, Hanım?" her husband asked.

Safiye Hanım explained every detail of the dream, and she even mentioned that she had smelled the aroma of the rose oil Hayriye Ana used.

"I would say it's a good dream," said Hikmet Efendi, "but just to be sure, let's relate it to Husnu *Baba** and see what he thinks."

Husnu Baba was a sheik who lived at a *tekke*** close to Kanlıca. He and Jamila's father had known each other since childhood. Although it was common for religious scholars to have reservations and sometimes outright antagonism towards sheiks and Sufism, Hikmet Efendi had high regard for Husnu Baba. Their religious paths were different: Hikmet Efendi had traveled an exoteric road, while Husnu Baba had followed an esoteric path. Jamila's father knew with certainty, however, that Husnu Baba was an enlightened and trustworthy man.

"Did you get any information from the ambassador in Paris?" Safiye Hanım asked curiously.

"I did, indeed," replied Hikmet Efendi. "Kamil's teachers were full of praise for his medical skills and his breeding. They said he has a great future before him. Everyone the Consulate spoke with had only good things to say about Kamil. What does Jamila think about all this? Is she making her usual objections?"

"Jamila is trying to hide her feelings, but I can see the light in her eyes every time Kamil's name is mentioned. I don't think there will be any objections this time," replied Jamila's mother.

"Then, if Husnu Baba reads the dream positively, I guess there is no reason to reject this proposal," Hikmet Efendi concluded, with a slight quiver in his voice.

---

* A term of adres to "father"

** Dervish hall.

Safiye Hanım looked at her husband. He had a smile on his lips, but she could see in his eyes his concern about giving in marriage their only child. Jamila had been their greatest blessing and joy in life. It was hard to even imagine their home without Jamila's laughter and enthusiasm. Whenever either of them had a physical ache or pain, it was Jamila who comforted and took care of them. Her compassion, like her other feelings, ran deep. She even took care of all the stray cats and dogs in the neighborhood or any bird that suffered from a broken wing. Her absence would leave a huge emptiness in their lives.

Also, there was the question of her happiness. Jamila's father and mother had always put their daughter's happiness first. Would Kamil always be able to put Jamila's interests before his own?

Safiye Hanım responded to her husband with the same quiver in her voice, "*Mevlam ne eylerse güzel eyler.*" *

The next day was Thursday. Kamil's father, Osman Efendi, sent word that he and Kamil's two uncles would be coming that evening to ask permission from Jamila's father for her hand in marriage. Hikmet Efendi had inquired after Husnu Baba the first thing that morning, but he learned that the sheik had gone to Mecca and wasn't expected back for another two months. He could not expect Kamil's family to wait that long, so he called Jamila to his study.

Tenderly looking his daughter in the eyes, Hikmet Efendi said softly to Jamila, "Osman Efendi and two of Kamil's uncles want to come this evening to ask for your hand in marriage. First I want to know what you think and feel about this marriage. *Canım kızım*,** is Kamil acceptable to you?"

Jamila blushed a little, but the conviction in her voice was clear: "Baba, I think Kamil is the man I have been waiting for. My heart tells me that he is."

---

* "Whatever God ordains is for the good."

** "My precious daughter."

Hikmet Efendi paused a moment, as if weighing something in his mind.

Then he replied, "If you are certain, Jamila, then all that is left for me is to support you in this decision and pray for the best for you. You have my blessings."

Jamila leaned over and kissed her father's right hand. Her father kissed Jamila on the forehead, and the matter was settled. Then he sent word to Osman Bey that they were welcome that evening.

Laden with gifts of sweets and cut flowers, Kamil's father and two uncles called on Hikmet Bey that evening after dinner. They asked for and received his consent to marriage between Jamila and Kamil. It was customary for elder males in the families to handle marriage agreements and arrangements on behalf of the young couple. Although they didn't discuss any details at this time, Hikmet Efendi invited all of Kamil's family to dinner a week later.

When the two families met the following week, the men and women dined separately. In the males' reception room Hikmet Efendi saw Kamil in person for the first time. He was not disappointed. Kamil's demeanor was both humble and self-assured at the same time. He immediately made people feel at ease with him, a valuable trait for a doctor.

It was again the elder males who discussed the details of the marriage arrangements. First of all, the issue of *mahr** was brought up. Kamil's father suggested a marriage settlement of 20,000 gold piasters, with half to be paid before the wedding and half to be deferred payment. Hikmet Efendi thought it was a generous sum, so he agreed without prolonging the discussion.

Then they discussed where the couple would reside. Again Osman Efendi took the lead. He recommended that Kamil and

---

* A mandatory marriage settlement paid by the groom to the bride. It was divided into two parts, the first of which was given to the bride before the consummation of the marriage and the second of which was pledged to be paid in case of divorce or death of the husband.

Jamila live with himself and Seniha Hanım in their family mansion in Beylerbeyi. Since Kamil was their only child, the mansion would be his anyway after their deaths. Until then, they wanted to spend their remaining years close to their son.

Hikmet Efendi welcomed this offer because it would mean that Jamila would remain near to her family home. Her parents would be close by in case she needed them. Tentatively Hikmet Efendi agreed, but first he wanted to discuss the issue with Jamila and her mother.

Meanwhile in the harem, Safiye Hanım and Jamila were hosting Seniha Hanım and the two wives of Kamil's uncles who had accompanied her. One of the women, Neslishah Hanım, was a beautiful Georgian who had served in the imperial harem before her marriage. Her stories about life in the palace intrigued Jamila, but she didn't want to seem too curious.

After dinner while the women were drinking coffee, Safiye Hanım called in one of her young slave women who was an accomplished lute player. After the *cariye* played several pieces skillfully, Neslishah Hanım asked if she could hold the lute. To Jamila and her mother's surprise, the *saraylı* began playing a difficult piece of Turkish classical music. Later Neslishah Hanım explained that she had been trained in the palace and had, in fact, played in the orchestra for five years.

Before the guests left Seniha Hanım invited Jamila's family to dinner at their house the following week. Jamila got Neslishah Hanım's promise that she would play the lute again then.

As soon as Hikmet Efendi entered the harem after the guests had left, Jamila looked expectantly at her father. He understood that she wanted his impression of Kamil.

"*Canım kızım*," said Hikmet Efendi, "I, of course, met Kamil this evening."

"Yes, Baba," Jamila eagerly replied.

Using an old Turkish saying, her father replied with a smile: "I think 'the pot rolled around and found its lid'" (meaning they were a perfect match).

"Really, Baba?" Jamila exclaimed. "Please tell me everything about him!"

Hikmet Efendi continued: "Well, Kamil is tall and handsome, but, more importantly, he appears to be a serious and intelligent young man. He has great respect for our traditions, on the one hand, but is open to innovation as well. And naturally he is cosmopolitan, having studied six years abroad."

"And will you be happy to call him your son, Baba?" asked Jamila.

"As long as he takes good care of my Jamila, I will be more than happy to call him my son," replied her father, stroking the young girl's hair.

Jamila thought her heart would burst. It was very important for her to have her parents' approval of Kamil. It made her feel sure she was making the right decision.

"*Kızım*, call your mother here so we can talk over some details," her father said to Jamila.

The young girl looked into the next room where she saw her mother sitting on a prayer rug. Safiye Hanım had just finished praying and was reciting God's *Esma ul-Husna* or Beautiful Names on her prayer beads. Jamila gave her a big hug and the two of them went to the reception room where Hikmet Efendi was waiting.

After Safiye Hanım sat down, Jamila's father told them about the amount of marriage settlement. The young girl's mother also thought it was a generous amount. She had not heard of a larger sum in her social circle.

When Hikmet Efendi told Jamila and her mother about Osman Efendi's suggestion that the young couple live with them in Beylerbeyi, he saw a look of relief on Safiye Hanım's face. She was pleased that her daughter would not be going far away.

"What do you think about living with your in-laws, Jamila?" asked her father.

"Baba, first of all, I'll be in easy visiting distance from you and Anne*, which makes me very happy. Secondly, Seniha Hanım is a very experienced and mature woman. She spent a lot of time in Europe while Kamil was studying in Paris. I'm sure she can teach me many things," responded Jamila.

When Safiye Hanım jokingly added, "I'm certain all the stray cats and dogs in Beylerbeyi will be happy about Jamila's moving there," they all broke into laughter.

The next afternoon the initial payment of Jamila's *mahr* was promptly sent to their home. Jamila's family responded by sending Kamil's family what was called the "engagement bundle," a set of presents for all members of the immediate family, including Kamil's uncles and their wives. The gifts, which also included fruit and candy, were wrapped in a beautifully embroidered satin cloth, tied in a bundle and taken to Kamil's home by Jamila's nursemaid, Gulshah.

As was custom, once Kamil's family received the "engagement bundle," they reciprocated with the "engagement set," which consisted of five large trays. Each tray was wrapped in a cloth and tied with a large ribbon. The trays contained flowers, fruit, preserves, spices, coffee, candy and henna. There were gifts for the whole family and special items for Jamila like bath accessories such as perfumes, ivory combs, wooden bath clogs inlaid with mother-of-pearl, a silver hand-mirror and a small, silver wash basin. One tray contained red velvet material for the wedding dress in addition to other dress material and, most importantly, a silver box with a small drawer in it containing a large diamond ring.

When Jamila and her parents went to the Beylerbeyi mansion for dinner, the men again discussed details of the wedding arrangements.

---

* Turkish for "mother"

It was decided that the official marriage would take place three months later at the bride's house, thus allowing time for preparations to be completed. As was the custom, a legal contract would be signed by the bride and groom. The contract, which would be recorded in court, would stipulate the amount and conditions of the *mahr*, the amount of *nafaka* or daily allowance to be paid to the bride for her personal needs and any other special conditions. The wedding celebration, which was a public affair, was to be held a few days after the official ceremony, and the marriage would not be consummated until that time.

In the large reception hall in the harem, Jamila glanced around at the room that was to be a part of her new home. The gently flowing water in the marble fountain was soothing to her ears. Looking out the window towards the straits, she saw a large sailboat gliding past. It was almost evening and the crimson sun appeared to be liquid gold melting behind the distant hills. Fishermen in small crafts were returning home with their day's catch. The Bosphorus seemed to have a spirit and vitality all its own. It was both enchanting and captivating. Jamila felt peaceful and content sitting in this room. She felt "at home" in her new home.

The women were discussing fashion and bridal dress models. Seniha Hanım described some white and pastel colored bridal gowns she had seen in Europe. This fashion had slowly begun to enter Istanbul society, but it was still very rare. Safiye Hanım praised the traditional red wedding caftan model that she and other Ottoman women had worn for centuries.

"Nothing could be more beautiful than a red caftan embroidered with gold or silver thread in the *bin dallı* (thousand branches) design," she said.

"And what does Jamila think?" asked Seniha Hanım.

"I agree with Anne," she replied. "I feel honored to wear the same style of dress my mother and grandmothers wore before me."

The other women agreed and the topic of conversation changed.

After dinner Neslishah Hanım kept her promise and played several compositions on the lute. A number of young slave girls also sang and danced for the guests in accompaniment to Turkish musical instruments. It was such a lovely evening, Jamila didn't really want to say good-bye, but custom dictated that they not stay too long. A bride-to-be should never appear overly eager.

The next day a flurry of activity began in Jamila's home. There were dresses to be sewn and trousseau items to be completed. Safiye Hanım was accomplished in the handicrafts of embroidery and lace-making, as were most Ottoman women. Ever since Jamila's birth, her mother had been preparing for this time. Dozens of sets of bed linens, pillow covers, towels, napkins, table cloths, underwear, scarves, handkerchiefs and countless other items had been skillfully and lovingly prepared for Jamila's trousseau. Now these were all taken out of the chests where they had been stored, aired, carefully controlled, and completed when necessary.

And, of course, the bridal dress had to be made. Jamila decided she wanted her wedding dress to be embroidered with silver thread and adorned with small pearls. A skillful Armenian seamstress was called in for that job and she set to work with the red velvet sent in the engagement set. All the female slaves helped with the trousseau according to their talents. Even neighbors came by to help. Jamila's home was buzzing with activity.

That evening after dinner Hikmet Efendi wanted to discuss which special conditions were to be added to the wedding contract. Turning to Safiye Hanım, he asked his wife:

"Hanım, do you have any suggestions regarding the marriage contract?"

"Yes, I do," replied Safiye Hanım. "I recommend that Jamila and Kamil not move outside of Istanbul. I think it's wise for Jamila to be close enough that we can support her in her time of need."

"Jamila, how about you? Do you have any special conditions?" asked her father.

"No, Baba," Jamila said. "I can't think of any."

"What about the stipulation that you will be divorced without losing your deferred *mahr* payment in case Kamil takes another wife?" asked Hikmet Efendi.

Taken aback a little, Jamila replied, "But, Baba, I thought very few men take a second wife. Isn't polygamy socially unacceptable?"

"Jamila, it is socially unacceptable unless the man's first wife is barren," responded her father, "but it is still legal for a Muslim man to take up to four wives. Unless you put a special condition in your marriage contract, Kamil would not be responsible for paying your deferred *mahr* in case you want a divorce."

Jamila could not imagine an enlightened person like Kamil taking another wife. But, on the other hand, she didn't want to oppose her father, so she agreed.

"Alright, Baba," she said, "if you think it's a good idea."

"Your father is right, Jamila," her mother said. "Many Ottoman women put this condition in their contracts. Besides, it's better to take precaution in time, than to be sorry later on."

Seeing that there were no other conditions, Hikmet Efendi suggested that they go to bed early because there was still much to be done.

Jamila was filled with mixed emotions as the days and weeks flew by. She had lived her whole life in the secure embrace of her parents. She had never had to ask for anything from them, for they always knew her needs in advance. Their concern and consideration for her had made Jamila's life an easy ride. Soon, however, she would be embarking on a new path with a man who was a stranger to her. The uncertainty as to what was in store for her made Jamila a little anxious and tense.

On the other hand, she felt a strong attraction towards Kamil although she had not yet spoken with him. Her heart had told Jamila that marrying Kamil was the right thing to do. Since there was no way for her to be certain that she was taking the right step, she could only trust her instincts that it would not lead to disappointment…

Chapter 3

Dolmabahce Palace, 1858

Sasa and the other three Circassian girls in the carriage were all under the age of ten. Not only were the slaves easier to be trained when they were young, but the period of service for young white girls was nine years, so youth was an advantage for being selected to serve in the royal palace. After they had served the appointed time, these young women were freed and given a legal document to that effect. If they had not attracted the attention of the Sultan or been selected as consorts to the princes, there were two roads open to them. Talented and capable young women could remain in the palace and move up in the administrative hierarchy or they could marry into the Ottoman ruling elite. Due to their training, social accomplishments and connections to the royal family, these girls were highly sought after as mates.

After a while the carriage turned off the main street and entered the palace grounds through the Valide Sultan's Gate. The horses came to a stop in front of the imperial harem. Rauf Efendi opened the carriage door and the four girls got out. Sasa had never seen such huge buildings. She felt a little overwhelmed. The girls passed two more black guards as they entered the imperial harem. They were met by a senior slave woman in her forties named Ferahshad Kalfa.

"Welcome to your new home, my little sisters. I hope you'll have a pleasant stay," said the kalfa, with a warm smile on her face. She spoke to the girls in a Circassian dialect.

She was dressed in a turquoise blue, brocade caftan with a gold floral design in it and wore a sheer silk blouse and yellow silk *shalvar** under her caftan. A small round velvet cap called a *hotoz* was perched on her head, and she wore a pearl necklace around her neck. Flat slippers decorated with sequins completed her outfit. Ferahshad Kalfa's demeanor was very dignified. She looked more like an aristocrat than a slave woman. Her manners were very refined as well.

As the girls were being led down the corridor, they saw several other young *cariye*s, all of whom were dressed in beautiful costumes. Smiling, the young women all welcomed the newcomers. The girls were taken to a large room that housed new slave girls in training. It was a light and spacious room with low, built-in Ottoman sofas on three sides of the room. There was a large wooden cupboard on the other side of the room that housed the bedding, among other things. Egyptian reed matting completely covered the wooden floor with a large Turkish carpet in the center of the room.

Shortly after the new girls arrived, two seamstresses and their assistants were summoned. New dresses were to be sewn immediately for the new arrivals. Their measurements were taken so the seamstresses could set to work. The girls were all given colorful satin *shalvar*s, beige linen shirts, embroidered vests and slippers to put on after they bathed. Then they were taken straight to the *hamam*.**

The Turkish bath consisted of two large rooms with grey marble fixtures. The first was called the "cool" room; it was where bathers got accustomed to the warm, steamy air of the bath before entering the other "hot" room. After coming out of the hot room, they also cooled down there before going back to the dressing room. Both rooms had large marble basins with hot and cold water running

---

* A kind of loose-fitting trouser worn under a caftan by both Ottoman men and women.

** Turkish hot bath.

from the spigots. A spacious dressing room was adjacent to the bath; bathers undressed there before entering the bath and got dressed there afterwards.

When Sasa and the other girls entered the dressing room, they were given large linen wraps to drape around their bodies. The attendant there showed them how to wrap themselves so as to cover their bodies from their chests to their knees. Then the girls went one by one behind a Chinese silk screen with large, colorful butterflies embroidered on it and, after undressing, wound the linen wraps around their bodies. Each girl was also given a small metal soap box with a handle on top for easy carrying and holes on the bottom for draining the soap. It contained a comb and a piece of raw silk cloth, as well as soap.

The attendant in the dressing room led the girls to the cool room and turned them over to two bath attendants who would help them bathe and wash their hair. The girls were thoroughly soaped, scrubbed, groomed and perfumed. The whole process took almost two hours. The "hot" room was almost too hot for Sasa; she could barely breathe there. Just when she thought she would faint, the attendant led her back into the "cool" room where her body temperature gradually dropped. However, when she looked at herself in the mirror in the dressing room, she could hardly recognize the bright-red, shiny face staring back at her. The girls got dressed and rested a while on the sofas in the dressing room, while they drank cool sherbet and ate fruit the attendant offered them.

After a short while, Mushfika Kalfa, a young slave woman in her mid-twenties, came to get the girls and take them back to their room. She was one of four junior kalfas assigned to oversee the twenty girls in the room where Sasa would stay. She was on duty with another kalfa, but they would be relieved by two other women the next week. After resting for one week, they would return to the same duty. Sasa liked the kind look in Mushfika Kalfa's deep blue eyes; it reminded her a little of the compassion in her mother's eyes.

When they returned to their room, the novice slave girls had not yet returned, but the other kalfa was there. Mushfika Kalfa introduced the young woman:

"This is Gulbahar Kalfa. Her name means 'spring rose.' Isn't she as lovely as a spring rose?"

Gulbahar Kalfa was dressed in a long pink dress that was fitted at the waist. Tiny pearl buttons extended from her collar all the way down the front to her hip line. There were three pieces to the dress skirt: one in the back and two separate panels in the front, with the side seams open to the hips. Underneath she wore white loose satin pants. Small rosebuds were braided into her long, dark hair and she wore bright pink slippers adorned with pearls and silver sequins. Looking at her with open admiration, the girls all agreed that she did, indeed, look as lovely as a spring rose.

"When girls first come to the Palace, they are always given a new, poetical name," continued Mushfika Kalfa. "What names shall we choose for these new *saraylıs*?" she asked, turning to the other kalfa.

"Look at these rosy cheeks," Gulbahar Kalfa said, smiling at the oldest of the girls. "Why don't we call her Gulizar (rosy-cheeked)?"

When the others looked at her, the girl blushed and the redness of her cheeks deepened even more.

Turning to the other two older girls, Mushfika Kalfa said, "How about Dilara (beloved) and Husnu-melek (beautiful angel)? Don't you think they are appropriate names?"

Gulbahar Kalfa agreed, and she congratulated the three girls on their new names. Then, turning to Sasa, she said:

"Look at the light in her face. Nothing will do for this little sister but Didenur! It means light of my eyes."

Sasa repeated the name to herself: Dee-de-noor. She liked the way it sounded and its meaning, as well. Shyly she smiled at Gulbahar Kalfa.

Then Mushfika Kalfa made a wish for all four girls: "May your new names be beneficial and auspicious!"

Shortly the rest of the girls, who were to be Didenur's new roommates, returned to their room. The new girls were introduced to the others, and they all began to get acquainted. However, there was no shouting or loud laughter, just a low buzz of conversation. Most of the girls were older than Didenur, but there was one other very young girl from Georgia around eight years of age. Her name was Servetseza (worthy of riches). Even at this young age she had a fierce kind of beauty. She was tall for her age and slender, with long, jet black hair and green eyes. The two young girls became instant friends, although they had some difficulty communicating because they didn't yet have a common language. Servetseza immediately began teaching Didenur new Turkish words.

At five o'clock several girls from the pantry service came in and began to set up dinner trays in the room. First they spread a large round cover with embroidered edges on the floor to catch any food that might be dropped. On top of that they placed a small, low table resembling a tripod, but with four folding legs. Another embroidered cloth was placed over the low table, and then a large tin-plated copper tray was set on top of that. Small cushions were placed around the edge of the first cover. This was repeated until five large dinner trays had been set up. Each girl had her own napkin and set of spoons, which she washed after every meal.

Large wooden trays of food were carried from the palace kitchen on the heads of the *tablakar*s or carriers and set on permanent benches in the entrance hall just inside the imperial harem. The food dishes on the trays had been wrapped and tied in a quilted cloth in the kitchen so the food wouldn't get cold. These trays were then distributed to the different rooms by girls in the food service. As they walked in unison down the corridors, this group of girls looked very smart in their immaculate white aprons embroidered around the edges.

In the rooms *kilercis* or pantry women oversaw the trays. Everyone washed their hands before sitting down by means of pitchers of water and basins brought in by attendants. One attendant poured the water, while another held the basin to catch the water. A third attendant held a towel for drying. The kalfas sat at a separate table and were served by girls assigned to their own service. The girls in training sat around the other four trays.

A salt cellar containing small bowls of salt, pepper and cinnamon was placed on each dinner tray, alongside a small carafe of fresh lemon juice. The dishes of food were placed in the center of the trays where everyone had access to them. There were no individual plates. It was the custom for everyone at the dinner tray to eat from these common dishes; it was believed that sharing the same dish would increase *baraqah* or abundance. The meal began with red lentil soup and was followed by flaky pastry filled with cheese, eggplant and mutton stew, stuffed grapevine leaves and then a rice dish. Compote made from dried apricots completed the meal.

Didenur noticed how delicately the girls were eating. They took very small bites and ate only from food directly in front of them. Also they dipped one edge of the spoon into the soup and put the other edge in their mouths. Just the right hand was used and there was no toying with food or reaching across the dinner tray. Everyone ate in silence as if they were performing a sacred act. After the meal Mushfika Kalfa made a prayer of thanks and then all the girls again washed their hands with the assistance of attendants pouring water over their hands into copper basins.

Servetseza continued teaching Didenur new Turkish words after they got up from the dinner tray. She began naming each of the items on the tray: salt (*tuz*), pepper (*biber*) and cinnamon (*tarçın*). Then she asked Didenur to repeat them. Servetseza couldn't help but giggle when, instead of repeating *tuz* for the word salt, Didenur called it *toz*, which means "dust" in Turkish. Learning her mistake, Didenur laughed, too.

The girls continued chatting quietly until the evening prayer, at which time gas lanterns were lit in the room and intricately embroidered prayer rugs were brought out of the large built-in closet and spread on the floor. Didenur didn't know how to make the ritual Muslim prayer, but Servetseza told her to just do the same things she did. Imitating her new Georgian friend, Didenur went through the motions of prayer. At the end one of the older girls recited some verses from the Quran. Although she couldn't understand what they meant, the sound of the chanting seemed to touch something deep within Didenur's soul. Somehow her heart felt more at peace.

After the prayer rugs were picked up and put back in the closet, the girls all sat down on the Ottoman sofas to listen to a story from Gulbahar Kalfa. Tonight's story was from Rumi's *Mathnawi*.

Scanning the room to make sure she had everyone's attention, Gulbahar Kalfa began:

"Tonight's story is about a mother elephant and her baby: Once upon a time in India a sage was walking down a dusty road when he saw a party of men. They were hungry, without provisions, and almost naked. They obviously had been traveling for a long time. The sage's heart opened up to them, and, after his greeting, he gave them some wise advice.

'I know,' he said, 'that you are anguished due to your hunger and emptiness. But, for God's sake, don't let your food be the young of the elephant! The elephant is in the direction you're headed, but don't tear in pieces its offspring. Heed my words!'

'The young elephants are on your road, and I know your hearts desire exceedingly to hunt them down.'

'They are very weak and tender and very fat, but their mother is searching for them and lying in wait.'

'She will roam a hundred miles distance in quest of her children, moaning and making lament.'

'Fire and smoke issue from her trunk: beware of hurting those cherished children of hers!'

'The sincere sage continued, 'Hearken to this counsel of mine, so that your hearts and souls may not be afflicted.'

'Be content with herbage and leaves; do not go in chase of the young elephants.'

'Now I have discharged my duty of warning you. I came to deliver this message, so that I may save you from fruitless repentance.'

'Beware! Let not greed waylay you!'

"The sage said this and then, after bidding them farewell, he left."

Gulbahar Kalfa halted for a moment to summarize in Circassian dialect what she had related so far, so that the newcomers could follow the story. Then she continued in Turkish:

"The famine and hunger of the men increased each step of the way.

"Suddenly, in the direction of a highroad, they saw a fat young elephant, newly born.

"They fell upon it like furious wolves, roasted it and ate it all up, and washed their hands.

"One of the travelers did not eat and pleaded with the others to abstain, because he remembered the sayings of the dervish.

"Those words prevented him from eating its roasted flesh old intelligence bestows new fortune.

"Then they all fell down and slept, except for the hungry one who was awake like the shepherd of a flock.

"He saw a frightful elephant approaching. First she ran towards him.

"She smelled his mouth three times: no disagreeable smell came from it.

"She paced around him several times and went off; the huge queen elephant did him no harm.

"She smelt the lips of every sleeper, and the smell of her young one's flesh was coming to her from each of those sleeping men.

"Each man had eaten of the roasted flesh of the baby elephant; the mother elephant quickly set about to tear them to pieces one by one. She had absolutely no fear.

"She tossed each man in the air recklessly, so that he dashed on the earth and then she trampled him under her foot.

***

"O bribe-eaters, you eat the young elephant. Know that the Master of the elephant will wring out your breath!... He does smell it, but He conceals the fact from us. The good and bad smells go up to heaven. While you are sleeping, the smell of that unlawful deed is beating on the blue sky... The smell of pride and the smell of greed and the smell of lust will become like the smell of onions when you speak. You swear that you haven't eaten onions and garlic, but the breath of your oath bears witness against you... Many prayers are rejected because of the smell..."*

The young *cariye*s had all listened to the story with keen and undivided attention. Gulbahar Kalfa summarized the rest of the story in Circassian dialect and then she asked the girls to tell the moral of the story in their own words. One of the older girls commented that the moral could apply to any sin. Another said that even if other people couldn't smell the stench of our sins, obviously our Creator could. The story had a powerful impact on Didenur, and in her heart she vowed to try and never attract "the rage of the mother elephant."

After trays of dried fruits and nuts were passed around, the prayer rugs were again brought out for the night prayer. This time as Didenur imitated the motions of Servetseza, she asked God to keep her soul's breath pure and clean.

After prayers, the beds were made up for the night. All the girls slept on separate mattresses that were kept stacked up in the large

---

* Rumi, Jalaluddin. *The Mathnawi of Jalaluddin Rumi, Book III*, trans. R. A. Nicholson (London: Messrs Lizac & Co. LTD, 1972) pp. 8-13.

closet during the day. In order to have full control of the room, the bed of each kalfa was located so as to have the beds of five girls on her right and five on her left. Didenur was glad to see that her bed had been put just next to Mushfika Kalfa's bed. A lamp was left burning all night long. Later a patrol of experienced *cariye*s called *katibe* kalfas would check the room several times during the night. It was their duty to make sure that nothing was amiss in the imperial harem.

In the very early hours of the morning Didenur began dreaming. Again she saw the fog surrounding her village, but this time it seemed different, less sinister. Didenur heard her mother's voice:

"My sweet daughter, don't worry about us. We are all well. Star is growing bigger and stronger every day. We miss you very much, but we place your future in God's trust."

Didenur suddenly roused from her sleep. She was disoriented for a moment and couldn't understand where she was. Then she saw Mushfika Kalfa sitting up on her bed making *zikir** with her prayer beads. The young woman leaned over towards Didenur, patted her on the head and told her to go back to sleep because it was still quite early. Comforted by both the kalfa and her dream, Didenur put her head back on the pillow and drifted off to sleep.

All the girls were woken up shortly before dawn to make the morning prayer. The beds were picked up and the room was put in order again. Then the girls began reading and studying the Quran. Those who were more advanced helped the others. Once a week their teacher listened to recitations. If a girl made her recitation well, she would get a new lesson for the next week. Didenur and the other newcomers began learning the Arabic alphabet and the shorter verses that are recited during ritual prayers. At first the Arabic letters seemed very strange to her, but before long she became familiar with them.

---

* Recitation of God's attributes.

After the religion lessons were over, Turkish lessons began. Again, the more advanced helped to tutor the others. When Servetseza finished her own lesson, she helped Didenur memorize new words. With a wide grin on her face, Servetseza asked her new friend what the word for salt was. This time Didenur got it right.

An hour's break for the morning meal was followed by a lesson in embroidery. Handeru Kalfa, their teacher, had brought a large bundle of embroidery pieces for the girls to use as models. There were pillow covers, towels, prayer rugs, table cloths, napkins, dresses and even underwear ornamented with the most exquisite flower designs roses, tulips, carnations, daisies and daffodils. Didenur was amazed by the skill with which these items had been decorated. She wondered if she would ever be able to make such beautiful works of art. After tracing a simple flower design on a small piece of material, Didenur began to embroider along the lines. It took her an hour to embroider a simple rose. When she finished, she was so disappointed that she pulled out the thread and started all over again. Servetseza told her not to be discouraged. Almost all the girls in the palace eventually became accomplished embroiderers.

Servetseza looked at Didenur with a gleam in her eye and said, "Do you know what we're going to do tonight?"

Didenur shook her head "no."

"Tonight there's a concert in the Valide Sultan's hall. The women of the royal family will probably all be there maybe even the Sultan!" exclaimed the little Georgian girl. "I can't wait!"

Didenur wondered if she had understood correctly. Might she really see the Sultan tonight?

That evening after dinner all the girls put on fancy dresses and gave careful attention to their hair. The kalfas helped the young *cariyes* look their best; after all these girls were in their charge and they wanted them to make the best possible impression on the royal family. Servetseza wore a long green silk dress that was trimmed with gold thread around the high collar, the sleeves and the hem of the dress. The shade of green just matched the color of her eyes. Gold beads were braided into her long black hair. Didenur wore one of the new dresses that had been sewn for her. It was a long royal blue silk dress with a quilted bolero jacket. Pearls were braided into two strands of her hair hanging on each side, while the rest of her hair fell free over her shoulders. When Didenur looked at herself in the mirror she could hardly believe her eyes. She had never owned or even seen such a beautiful dress in her village.

The kalfas escorted the girls upstairs at seven o'clock. They joined a large crowd of other *cariye*s who had already arrived and were sitting on the floor on a large piece of cloth spread out at one end of the large hall. Because of their young age, Servetseza and Didenur were allowed to sit in front of the older girls along with several other young slave girls. Didenur looked around at the splendid hall in astonishment. It was lit up brilliantly by means of a magnificent crystal chandelier hanging in the center of the ceiling. There were standing chandeliers in the four corners of the hall, as well. The ceiling of the hall was elaborately decorated in the Baroque style. Chairs and sofas were upholstered in bright crimson brocade with a large beige floral design in it, and the curtains were made from matching red and beige striped silk material. Huge mirrors hung in gold enameled frames on two sides of the room. An enormous beige and crimson Turkish carpet covered most of the wooden parquet floor, which had a geometrical design. Large Chinese porcelain vases with cut flowers in them stood on elegant consoles decorated with inlaid mother-of-pearl.

In one corner of the room the Sultan's four wives and three *iqbals** were seated on chairs according to their rank of First Lady (*Kadın Efendi)*, Second Lady, etc. Two of his daughters were present, too: Hamide Sultan (ten years old) and Aliye Sultan (seven years old). The royal consorts and princesses were all elegantly dressed. Most

---

* Royal consorts of a lower rank than the royal wives.

were wearing traditional Turkish costumes, but two of the women and Princess Aliye were dressed according to Western fashion. All of the women were adorned with costly jewels such as diamonds, rubies and emeralds. The Sultan's wives were beautiful Circassian women who had at one time entered the imperial harem as young slave girls. Having undergone rigorous training and grooming, they had become worthy of their exalted position. Although these women did not have the legal status of wives, they were socially accepted as wives and they had all the prestige and respect that accompany such a high office.

A chamber orchestra of *cariye*s with both eastern and western instruments occupied the corner across from the royal women. Slave girls in the palace with natural musical talent were taught and trained by the best Ottoman musicians of the time. The female musicians were seated on small cushions placed on the carpet. They were all wearing long brocade caftans in different colors with loose-fitting, satin pants underneath. They had small caps shaped like a fez on the top of their heads with transparent silk scarves trailing down from them. Didenur thought they looked like a bouquet of spring flowers.

The Chief *Haznedar* or Treasurer entered the room to announce the arrival of the Sultan. Everyone in the room stood up. The Sultan was accompanied by his mother, the Valide Sultan. When the Sultan entered the hall, all the women present -except for his mother- made a *temenna** and a deep bow of reverence. He greeted the royal women one-by-one and then took his seat on a special sofa reserved for him. The Valide Sultan and the princesses sat to his right and the royal consorts sat to his left according to their rank. Didenur looked at the Sultan carefully. He was slightly built, had large brown eyes and appeared to be in his middle thirties. He acted very courteously towards the royal women. The Sultan

---

* An Ottoman greeting that is made by raising the right hand first to the lips and then to the forehead.

was wearing a uniform in a western cut, but it had a great deal of gold ornamentation on the jacket. His buttons and the stones on his jacket collar were sparkling diamonds, and he wore a plain red fez on his head.

The Sultan made a motion with his hand, and the musicians began playing their instruments. After the orchestra played five classical Turkish arrangements, a brief intermission was given and coffee was served first to the Valide Sultan and Sultan and then to the royal consorts. The girls in the coffee service skillfully and elegantly brewed the coffee in a gold coffee pot on a small brazier held by one of them. The coffee was poured into fine porcelain cups which were placed on inlaid gold saucers decorated with small, precious stones. The coffee ceremony was intriguing to Didenur, as was everything else going on this evening. After the cups were collected the concert continued with three western classical pieces. At the end of the program, the Sultan congratulated the musicians, and the Chief *Haznedar* gave them gifts of money from the imperial purse. Speaking with the royal women for a short time, the Sultan then retired to his quarters nearby. The royal women followed suit and then the *cariye*s left as well. Didenur took one last look at the hall before she left. The brilliance of the lights was reflected in the large mirrors on the walls, giving the whole room a magical aura.

The next day Didenur was still under the spell of the previous evening. Throughout her morning classes, she thought more about the concert and the royal family than her lessons. The other girls, too, exchanged their impressions about the concert at every opportunity. When it was time for the morning meal, Mushfika Kalfa called Didenur and Servetseza aside.

"I have some wonderful news for you two, my little sisters," said the kalfa beaming a large smile on her face.

"What is it?" both girls asked in unison.

"Princess Aliye's mother has sent word that she wants to see both of you. She saw you last night at the concert, and she is hoping you might be suitable companions for Aliye Sultan. If she and the princess approve of you, you'll go to their apartment every afternoon to keep the princess company. Eat your meal now and then I'll take you to their quarters."

Both girls were elated. They were so excited they could hardly finish their meal. After Didenur and Servetseza put on their best dresses and touched up their hair again, Mushfika Kalfa took them upstairs to the princess' quarters. Aliye Sultan lived with her mother Tiryal *Hanım* (Lady) in a private apartment on the second floor of the imperial harem. The girls were shown into an anteroom, which was basically furnished with western furniture. The sofa and chairs were upholstered in antique gold silk material. A large gold and green Turkish carpet was spread on the wooden parquet floor. In the middle of the room there was a large silver brazier with a brass cover, which was used for heating the room in cold weather. Oil paintings of natural scenes adorned the walls. A crystal pitcher and glasses on a silver tray were sitting on a small console next to an Iznik vase full of cut flowers.

Three other rooms and a bathroom branched off from the main room. One of the rooms was the princess' bedroom. It had a large four-post bed with white curtains enclosing it. The bedspread was made from red silk with an intricate tulip design embroidered in gold thread. On top of the bed there was a canopy that had a large crown on top designating that it was the bed of a princess. Another of the rooms was the bedroom of the princess' mother. Along with a bed, couch and dressing table, there was a bookcase on one wall. As was true for most of the other consorts, Tiryal Hanım spent much of her spare time reading. The third room was used as a sitting room. The fourth door led to a grey marble bathroom where the bathing area and toilet were divided into two separate spaces. Next to the bathroom door there were a number of what appeared to be closet doors, but actually they concealed stairways leading both upstairs and downstairs. The head kalfa and a number of other kalfas in the service of the royal consort and the princess lived downstairs. By means of the stairway, they had access to the royal quarters without having to use the main staircase of the imperial harem.

The first thing Didenur noticed as she entered the anteroom was the piano standing next to the wall. She had no idea how it was used. The kalfa who opened the door asked them to wait a minute while she informed Tiryal Hanım and Aliye Sultan of their arrival. The kalfa came back and led them into Aliye Sultan's bedroom where the princess and her mother were sitting on a small couch. As soon as Mushfika Kalfa and the two girls entered the room, they bowed deeply before the royal consort and princess and made the Ottoman *temenna*. Pointing to some red velvet cushions on the floor, Tiryal Hanım asked them to be seated.

Aliye Sultan was dressed in a short, western-style navy blue crepe dress with a little row of white lace around the collar. Her hair was cut short in a rather boyish crop. She had dark eyes, dark brown hair and light skin. When Didenur looked up at her, the princess' face broke into a wide smile.

"Anneciğim, are these my new playmates?" asked the princess, before Mushfika Kalfa had a chance to introduce the girls.

"If you want them to be," replied her mother.

"I do want them, I do. Let's begin playing at once!" exclaimed the little princess. She hopped off the couch, took Didenur and Servetseza by the hand and led them to the piano. She sat down and began to play a simple melody. Didenur was mesmerized by the sound. She couldn't help but hope in her most inward heart that one day she, too, would be able to play this extraordinary instrument.

A little later Aliye Sultan's governess asked the girls if they would like to paint some pictures. They all said yes and sat down at a small table in the princess' room. The governess brought a large sketch pad of paper and water colors that had recently been brought from Europe. The three girls each diligently applied themselves to painting the best picture they could. Aliye Sultan painted a peacock that lived in the palace gardens. Servetseza painted a patch of tulips, and Didenur painted Star as she imagined him to look.

Another kalfa brought in some lemonade and sesame sticks for the girls. After they finished the refreshments, Mushfika Kalfa asked permission for them to leave.

"You have my permission to leave," said the sprite princess, "but only on one condition."

"And what is that, my sultan?" asked Mushfika Kalfa.

"You have my permission to leave only if you promise that Didenur and Servetseza can come back tomorrow," replied Aliye Sultan with a large grin on her face.

"It appears to be decided," said the princess' mother. "From now on we'll expect the girls every afternoon."

Taking their leave, Mushfika Kalfa and the two girls bowed respectfully and left the royal apartment. Although no one spoke in the hallway of the imperial harem, the kalfa saw the joy in the girls' eyes. "How fortunate are these little *saraylıs*," thought the junior kalfa. "A close association with a princess is not the fate of many girls!"

Didenur continued her lessons in religion, the Turkish language and harem etiquette each morning, and then went everyday with Servetseza to visit Aliye Sultan in the afternoons. The three girls were being taught to embroider by one of the junior kalfas in the princess' service. Also, twice a week Didenur and Servetseza accompanied Aliye Sultan to her piano lesson, which was being given by a senior kalfa who had studied under a famous French musician. That was Didenur's favorite time; the music seemed to lift her spirit to another plane.

Today Aliye Sultan, Didenur and Servetseza were allowed to play outside in the harem garden. The princess' governess turned the girls over to one of the harem guards at the palace door. It was a warm summer day. The smell of jasmine and the cries of seagulls filled the air. Enjoying the dense greenery, Didenur had become lost in thoughts about her homeland and the events of the past several months. Suddenly Servetseza's voice brought her back to the moment.

"Look, look!" exclaimed Servetseza. "It's the peacock in Aliye Sultan's picture!" Didenur and the princess looked in the direction Servetseza was pointing. A beautiful blue-green peacock had fully spread its feathers and was proudly strutting in front of the girls as if to get their attention.

"Wait a minute, Servetseza," said the princess. "If that's the peacock in my picture, then what is it doing here?"

The three girls simultaneously burst into laughter. The peacock appeared to be offended by their laughter, because it abruptly closed up its tail feathers and ran back into the bushes.

CHAPTER 4

Beylerbeyi, 1858

While the carriage conveying Jamila and two of her kalfas advanced towards Rabia's mansion where women from the Ottoman elite were preparing a trousseau for a poor neighborhood girl, Jamila continued recollecting the events after her engagement to Kamil:

The day of the official marriage ceremony finally arrived. The local imam had gotten permission to marry the couple from the *kadı* (judge) and had come to Hikmet Efendi's home on Thursday afternoon. Jamila, her mother and Seniha Hanım waited in an adjacent room with the door open. The marriage contract was to be signed in the presence of the imam and two male witnesses. Kamil looked on as the proceedings began.

Before the signing, the imam read the conditions of the contract aloud, including the two conditions Hikmet Efendi requested. When the imam asked Jamila if she consented to the marriage, she replied "Yes." Then Jamila and Kamil and the imam all signed the contract, which would be legally registered by the imam.

This simple ceremony was followed by a sumptuous dinner for both families, the imam and the witnesses, but with the men and women dining separately, of course. Although Jamila and Kamil were now officially married, they would remain strangers to one another until the commencement of the public wedding feast.

That night after the dinner was over and her parents had gone to bed, Jamila lay wide awake in her bed. She could hardly believe that she was now an officially married woman. Jamila wondered what Kamil was thinking and feeling. Did he long to look into her eyes as she longed to look into his? If only she could be together with him now… But custom and tradition did not allow it. Jamila would have to be a little more patient.

On Monday of the next week Jamila's trousseau was carried from her family home in Kanlıca to her new home in Beylerbeyi by means of a colorful bridal procession. Numerous male servants carried on their heads large wicker baskets filled with towels, cushions, scarves, fabrics, vases, china, etc. all small household items. Others carried trays of fruit, flowers and sweets. Each container was wrapped in bright gauze material tied with large red ribbons. Horses and mules carried bed mattresses, carpets and other large household items. Heavy articles like trunks of linen and clothing and metal braziers were transported in ox-drawn carts.

Following in the rear were several carriages of Jamila's friends and female relatives and, of course, her nursemaid, Gulshah, who was in charge of overseeing the trousseau display at the bride's new home. As the procession slowly wound along the narrow coastal road, on-lookers and bystanders made well-wishes and prayers for the new couple. Some youngsters blocked the way of the procession until they were given small coins, as was the custom. Money was always distributed generously during all marriage celebration activities to win the hearts and prayers of the people.

When the procession arrived at the Beylerbeyi mansion, Jamila's trousseau was carried into the two-room bridal suite that had been set aside for Kamil and his new bride. Two rooms with a magnificent view of the Bosphorous straits had been prepared for the couple. A small, private bath had been added, as well.

Gulshah Dadı oversaw the arrangement of the furnishings and the display of the bridal trousseau. As was custom, in one room all of Jamila's new clothing, linens, towels, covers, scarves, divan covers, silver coffee set, eating utensils, basins with ewers, and hand mirrors were attractively displayed for the perusal of the female guests. There were also a number of pieces of jewelry, which had been given as bridal gifts from close relatives and family friends. These were displayed under glass cases tied together with ribbons so that the jewelry could be seen, but the cases could not be opened.

In a corner in the other room a canopy was made of Jamila's silk scarves and embroideries and garlands of crepe flowers under which she would sit to receive, first, her husband and then all the female guests on Thursday. By evening the rooms had been fully furnished and prepared for the bride and groom and the wedding celebration soon to take place there.

Tuesday was the day of the bridal bath. Jamila, Safiye Hanım, Gulshah Dadı and a dozen or so female servants went to the large Turkish bath early in the morning. Jamila spent several hours in the bath being soaped, scrubbed, shampooed and perfumed. A special herbal concoction was massaged into her scalp to make her hair healthy and lustrous.

When Jamila left the hot room, Gulshah Dadı was waiting for her in the cool room to braid her hair. The nursemaid couldn't prevent tears from welling up in her eyes as she braided Jamila's hair. After all, it was she who had combed and braided Jamila's hair since she was a very little child. She silently prayed that her precious charge's future would be full of happiness. The task of braiding took about a half an hour, and then Jamila returned to the large dressing room where all her guests were waiting.

There was a great commotion there, with gypsy music and dancers and the excited chatter of the women and girls. Wearing her dressing gown which was richly embroidered with gold thread around the edges, Jamila kissed the hands of the women and the cheeks of her peers. They, in turn, offered their congratulations. After putting on a peach colored silk dress which she would wear until she put on her bridal dress, Jamila was led to the bridal throne made from pastel gauze material and ribbons. Seated like a queen, she watched the gypsy dancers' entertainment. After their performance ended, refreshments were served.

Although it was late afternoon, everyone was reluctant to leave the radiant bride. A trip to the Turkish bath was always a pleasurable social experience for women—a time for them to see old friends and catch up on the latest news. Today, however, was even more special. The atmosphere was full of best wishes and high hopes for Jamila. Many of the women there had known her since she was a child and they wanted only the best for her. They were all happy and proud to share in Jamila's passage from girlhood to womanhood.

Early in the afternoon on Wednesday, Jamila and her mother hosted Seniha Hanım, her female relatives and friends. The women guests were met at the door and escorted into the large reception room in the harem. There they were served coffee and Turkish delight. Shortly thereafter Jamila was escorted into the room and kissed the hands of all the women, beginning with Kamil's mother. After briefly sitting next to her mother-in-law, Jamila was escorted out of the room. The guests remained, however, to watch entertainment by female musicians and dancers. The lively music and exuberant performance of the dancers heightened the excitement of the wedding celebration. As the guests were leaving, Jamila came to the door to see them off. They all tossed coins over her head into the streets for the vendors and children there who had been patiently waiting for this moment.

That evening was the henna night, a time when Jamila said farewell to her girlhood. After all the female friends, relatives and neighbors of both the bride and groom were assembled in the reception hall, Jamila was escorted into the room by a long procession of her young unmarried friends. The girls were all elegantly dressed in beautiful dresses. Their hair was decorated with jewels and flowers, and they were carrying lighted candles in their hands. The bridesmaids sang solemn, traditional bridal songs as they accompanied Jamila. Shortly, however, the music and songs lightened up and dancers came in to entertain the guests.

While trays of every kind of imaginable dried fruit and nuts were being served, Jamila was escorted out of the room by two of her attendants. She took off her silk dress and put on a linen shirt and satin *shalvar*. Wearing a red veil over her face, Jamila was escorted back into the room and seated on a chair in the middle of the room. A thick paste of henna was applied to the palm of her right hand, and Seniha Hanım placed a large gold coin in it. The other guests followed suit. Then henna was applied to Jamila's other hand, after which small bags were placed over both hands until the henna set. Singing and dancing continued until most guests took their leave. Many of Jamila's childhood friends remained for the night. They stayed up talking with Jamila until very early in the morning, thus spending Jamila's last night of girlhood together.

The next morning Safiye Hanım, Gulshah Dadı, Jamila's friends who had spent the night and the female servants all helped get the bride ready. First Jamila put on a sheer white silk blouse that was adorned with small silver sequins and a red silk *shalvar* embroidered with silver thread around the waist and the trouser legs. Safiye Hanım helped Jamila put on her crimson red velvet caftan that had been worked all over with silver thread and small white seed pearls in an elegant branch design. Two servants pulled on her calfskin boots which were also adorned with silver thread and pearls. Gulshah Dadı assisted Jamila in putting her jewelry on--a necklace of precious stones and matching earrings given to her by Kamil's family, and more than twenty gold bracelets which were gifts from relatives on both sides. On her fingers she wore a large ruby ring, a gift from her mother and father, in addition to her wedding ring.

Jamila sat down on a sofa and Gulshah Dadı brushed her long dark hair and made eight braids that hung down in back. Long strands of silver called bridal tinsel were woven into each braid.

When her hair was ready, Jamila's friends made what is called "face decoration." First they whitened Jamila's face with powder and applied rouge on her cheeks. After that a fine line of *sürme* (eye-liner) was applied. Then they attached tiny precious stones to her forehead, cheeks and chin. Next came her long, red tulle bridal veil embroidered in silver thread, which extended down over her bridal dress. A silver filigree *tepelik* or bridal headdress with gems mounted in the interstices was placed on top of her head over the veil. Arrayed in her bridal apparel, Jamila was stunning.

Taking her daughter's arm, Safiye Hanım led Jamila into Hikmet Efendi's study. He was seated, reading the Quran. When he saw Jamila, he stood up and looked at her as if he were seeing her for the first time. Jamila was no longer his sweet little girl; she had become a striking young woman.

It was time for Hikmet Efendi to perform his last duty for his daughter before she left her father's house: the ceremony of the bridal girdle. Jamila knelt down and kissed her father's hand. He raised her up and girded her with an exquisite silver filigree belt with two large rubies on the belt clasp. The belt had been her mother's. Safiye Hanım wore it when she was a bride. There were tears in everyone's eyes, tears mixed with both joy and sorrow. Life would never be the same again for any of them. Safiye Hanım and Hikmet Efendi were sending their beloved daughter to a new, unchartered stage in her life-journey.

Speaking with difficulty, her father said, "*Canım kızım*, I entrust you to God's care."

"And I entrust both of you to God's care, as well," replied Jamila.

No more words were spoken; there was no need for them.

Meanwhile, a large party of Kamil's relatives had arrived to claim the bride and escort her to her new home. Kamil's father and male relatives were on horseback and the ladies were in carriages. They all came into the house for refreshments. After polite exchanges had been made, the party escorted Jamila to the bridal carriage. Gulshah Dadı was seated next to Jamila. As representative of the bride's family, she had an important role to play in the newlywed's first night.

The bridal procession slowly wound along the coastal road between Kanlıca and Beylerbeyi. Large, colorful scarves tied around all the horses' necks and the drum rolls of drummers accompanying the group heralded the approach of a new bride. The afternoon sun was sparkling on the Bosphorus waters, adding brilliance to an already perfect day. Again children and beggars blocked the procession at intervals along the way, and coins were distributed to them generously.

As the procession advanced, the sorrow of leaving her parents and childhood home began to fade as Jamila thought about Kamil and their new life together. She felt a warm glow in the pit of her stomach. When the bridal procession reached its destination, Kamil was waiting at the garden gate. The bridal carriage pulled in front of the mansion and Kamil opened the door, took Jamila's arm and helped her step down. Gulshah Dadı also got out of the carriage and Jamila walked between the two of them through the large crowd of women who had gathered to wait for the bride. Jamila could feel the warmth of Kamil's hand on her arm through the sleeve of her bridal dress. Although her heart was pounding, the new bride appeared to be calm and composed. They entered the house and Kamil and Gulshah Dadı escorted Jamila to the bridal chamber. Gulshah Dadı remained at the door of the room to give the couple a few minutes alone together before the female guests came in.

Kamil led Jamila to the bridal throne that had been prepared for her on Monday by her friends and relatives. After Jamila sat down, he lifted up her veil and looked intently into her eyes.

"I have been waiting for this moment since I first heard about you," Kamil said softly. "Jamila, you're even more beautiful than I imagined."

Then he took a large diamond with a clasp from his pocket and attached it to Jamila's hair. It was custom for the groom to give his bride a gift in token of his appreciation for seeing her face for the first time. Kamil leaned forward and was about to kiss the bride when Gulshah Dadı knocked on the door indicating that Jamila's guests had arrived. Kamil took leave of Jamila, but promised to return as soon as possible. Jamila felt as if her heart would melt when he looked into her eyes as he left to host his male guests in the *selamlık*.

The crowd of women all bearing wedding gifts poured into the rooms. Each individually congratulated the new bride, and she thanked them for coming and for their gifts. The women, most of whom were neighbors, all examined Jamila's trousseau and made complimentary remarks about it. Coffee and wedding candy were served to all the guests. After two hours of public display, Jamila went to a large sitting room where female family and friends were dining and being entertained with music. She kissed the hands of her mother and mother-in-law and then individually thanked all the guests for coming and accepted their congratulations.

Kamil was performing a similar ceremony in the male quarters where colleagues, friends and relatives were feasting and being entertained. Having finished their meal, many men sat around drinking Turkish coffee in small, elegant porcelain cups and smoking water pipes. Hot coals for the pipes were being carried by dozens of male servants dressed in black loose fitting pants, black vests and white shirts with colorful red striped shawls wrapped around their waists and red fezs on their heads. The aroma of freshly brewed coffee and fruit flavored tobacco filled the air. In one corner of the large room a group of musicians were playing Turkish string instruments, drums and tambourines.

When the evening call to prayer was heard from the minaret of a nearby mosque, all the men got up and went to perform the prayer together. There the festivities and celebration were left behind and rich and poor alike, side-by-side, all bowed down solemnly before God and performed the ritual prayers together. The Quranic recitation after the prayer had never sounded so beautiful to Kamil's ears. When the prayer ritual was complete, all the guests returned to the celebration. Amidst congratulations and well-wishes, Kamil kissed the hands of his father and father-in-law, took leave of his guests and returned to the bridal chamber.

Jamila had also returned and was sitting on her bridal seat with Gulshah Dadı close by. When Kamil entered the room, Gulshah Dadı got up and joined Kamil's hand to Jamila's and said, "May you grow old together on the same bed pillow." Then she excused herself and went to prepare a light meal for the couple.

Kamil took Jamila's hand and kissed it.

"Jamila, I hope I will be able to make you happy," Kamil said looking deeply into his bride's eyes.

"You already have," replied Jamila softly.

"When I was studying in Paris," continued Kamil, "I often dreamed of returning to Istanbul, marrying and raising a family. It motivated me to work and study, even when I didn't want to." Smiling, he said, "You see, you were a source of inspiration for me even before I met you."

Jamila smiled, too. She was curious about his life before they met. "Tell me about your life in France. Was it very difficult for you to live in a foreign country?" she asked.

Kamil began relating his experiences abroad and asking Jamila questions about her past life, too. Before they knew it, there was a knock on the door. Gulshah Dadı entered with soup, several vegetable dishes prepared in olive oil, yogurt and milk pudding. She set up a dining tray, saw to it that everything they needed was there, and then left them alone again.

Jamila ate very little. She felt a fullness that had nothing to do with food. She wondered if Kamil had the same feeling, but she was too shy to ask him. He ate little, as well, and soon the both of them got up from the dining tray. Kamil spread out a prayer rug prepared especially for him on the floor. It was custom for bridegrooms to perform a special prayer on their wedding night. While Kamil was praying, Gulshah Dadı came in and removed the tray. She told Jamila she would be back to help her get out of her wedding dress after the bride had performed the final ritual prayer of the day.

Although she appeared to be calm and collected, Jamila was both nervous and excited. She had to force herself to concentrate during the prayer.

In a short while Gulshah Dadı returned to help Jamila undress. They went into the other room where the bridal bed had been prepared with heavily embroidered sheets and pillowcases and covered with a white silk quilt worked all over with sequins and pearls. Gulshah Dadı carefully removed the bridal headdress and veil and laid them aside. Then she took Jamila's caftan, blouse and *shalvar* and hung them in a way that they would not get wrinkled, because Jamila would wear them again for the next two days when appearing before guests.

The dadı helped Jamila put on her bridal nightgown and robe which had been prepared for this occasion. The gown was made from red satin that draped the body, while the robe was of white silk with a design of red rosebud sprays. Both were trimmed with red lace, and the robe had a long, flowing train in the back. Gulshah Dadı unbraided Jamila's hair and brushed it over her shoulders.

Looking at the captivating bride with both concern and compassion, Gulshah Dadı said, "Jamila, I'll be sleeping in the room next to your suite. If you have even the slightest problem, I am here to help you as I have always been."

Jamila hugged her dear nursemaid. She was comforted by the close presence of a woman who was ready to give her life for Jamila without a second thought.

"God willing, I won't need any help, Dadı, but if I do, you are the one I'll turn to," replied Jamila with a grateful look on her face.

Gulshah Dadı went back into the other room, said good-night to Kamil and left the bridal suite.

Jamila stood up when Kamil entered the room and helped him off with his jacket and tie. She was full of mixed emotions. On the one hand, she was shy because Kamil was the first man she had ever been alone with except her father. But, on the other hand, she was falling in love with Kamil and being alone with him seemed very natural to her.

Sensing his bride's apprehension, Kamil asked, "Are you afraid, Jamila?"

"A little," she replied.

Caressing her face, Kamil said, "Don't be afraid, Jamila, you're in safe hands…"

The next morning Jamila was sitting in front of a window looking out at the straits. It was very early; the sun was just beginning to rise. The water looked like a huge, still sheet spread out before her; she couldn't see even a single ripple. Only the seagulls broke the surface calm when they dove down into the water to catch fish. There was a solemnity, a sanctity at this time of the day that was reflected in the straits. Shortly, with the ascendancy of the sun, everything would come to life again, but for now there was only a sacred silence. Jamila thought about the previous night. She felt she was the luckiest woman in the world to have a husband like Kamil. Just as she had known from the time she first saw his picture, he was very strong, but very gentle. In her heart the new bride thanked her Creator for this extraordinary blessing. After contemplating the scenery in front of her a little longer, Jamila returned to Kamil's side in bed.

A knock at the door aroused the newlyweds around ten o'clock. Gulshah Dadı brought in coffee for the two of them and said that both families were waiting for them. She closely scrutinized Jamila's face for any sign of uneasiness, but the new bride's broad smile reassured her that everything was all right. The dadı left for a half an hour to give the couple time to drink their coffee and to allow Kamil to get dressed. Then she returned to help Jamila dress and comb her hair.

The newlyweds left their suite and went to attend the banquets in their honor. Before going to host male relatives in the *selamlık*, Kamil paid his respects to his mother and mother-in-law. Again the couple was carefully scrutinized for any indication of incompatibility between them. Before Jamila and her mother entered the harem reception hall, Safiye Hanım questioned her daughter:

"Jamila, you look like a happy bride," said her mother.

"Anneciğim, I couldn't be happier," Jamila replied.

"Then your stars are compatible?" asked Safiye Hanım.

"More than compatible," the new bride responded.

"*Canım kızım*, I'm so relieved to hear that. Last night your father and I prayed for you all night long."

Mother and daughter embraced each other and then they went into the banquet room, which was filled with female relatives from both sides of the family. Today was the traditional "feast of sheep trotters" that was always held on the second day of marriage celebrations. The aroma of food reminded Jamila that she had hardly eaten anything during the last twenty-four hours. When the flurry of congratulations subsided, she was able to assuage her hunger a little before it was time to go back to her bridal throne to receive guests again.

Kamil hosted guests in the male quarters while Jamila received women in the bridal suite. The wedding festivities were open to rich and poor, alike. As brides and their trousseaus were always a subject of curiosity for most women, almost all those who heard about the wedding came to view the bride and extend their best wishes. From time to time Jamila's thoughts drifted away from her guests to Kamil, and she felt a warm glow in the pit of her stomach. Towards evening the final guests left and Jamila relaxed until Kamil returned from performing the evening prayer at the mosque. After a light meal with Kamil's parents, the couple retired to the bridal suite.

Taking his new bride into his arms, Kamil asked, "Jamila, I've been with guests all day long, but my heart has been with you. Were you thinking of me, too?"

Nodding her head, Jamila succumbed to Kamil's kisses and the intoxication of love. The meaning of "Kamil" is "perfection," and he was fully that in Jamila's eyes – flawless and faultless. He was everything Jamila had ever dreamed of in a man. She blindly and totally surrendered to him – body, mind and soul.

The next morning the couple again dressed in their wedding finery and started out to host the final day of feasting and festivities. Again friends and relatives of both the bride and groom's families came to celebrate the marriage and share the joy and hopes of the new couple and their families. Special occasions like marriage, births, circumcisions and holy pilgrimage were always celebrated publicly in Ottoman society. The well-wishes and prayers of the community added meaning and significance to milestones in human life.

By evening everyone was exhausted – the guests, the newlyweds and their families – but it was a sweet weariness. All the preparations, arrangements and expenditures had been worthwhile. It was a wedding that would not be soon forgotten.

After all the guests had left and the couple had paid their respects to Kamil's parents, they returned to their suite. On this evening they talked for hours in bed about their past experiences, Kamil's work, his activities in France and their hopes and aspirations. Jamila was pleased to learn that they thought similarly on many issues. She also learned that Kamil had future political ambitions. He was hoping to become the Sultan's chief physician one day, but for now he was eager to gain experience in his new position at the palace school.

The couple slipped off to sleep in each other's arms as they did every night during their first year of marriage. They had no quarrels or even serious differences of opinion. Most of their ideas were compatible and, in the few cases where they disagreed, Jamila always bowed to Kamil's decisions due to her love and respect for him.

Shortly after their first wedding anniversary Kamil gave his parents and Jamila some unexpected news at the dinner table:

"There has been a serious outbreak of cholera in the Black Sea region. I've been asked to head a medical team to combat the problem before it becomes an epidemic. If everything goes according to schedule, I'll be sailing to Trabzon two days from now."

Jamila's face clouded over. She knew there was a serious risk in treating cholera patients.

"Of course, my son," said Osman Efendi, "you must respond to the call of duty. How long will you be gone?"

"If everything goes well, I should be back in six to eight weeks," Kamil replied.

"We will miss you dearly," Seniha Hanım said, "but if you can help those poor souls suffering from cholera, then you must do your best. Also don't worry about us and Jamila. We'll be fine until you get back."

That night when they were alone, Jamila opened the subject of Kamil's trip to Trabzon again.

"Sevgilim, I can't bear the thought of being separated from you for so long. Couldn't I come with you? I could help care for the sick," Jamila suggested.

"Canım," Kamil replied, "We will be working very long hours under extremely difficult conditions. Of course, we won't only be treating patients in Trabzon; we will be traveling to outlying villages, as well. I wouldn't think of putting you under such conditions. The best thing you can do to show your love for me is to stay here with my parents where I know you will be safe and well cared for."

"But I'm sure I could be of help," Jamila insisted.

"No, my love," Kamil responded, "please understand." Trying to comfort Jamila, he added, "Besides, I will be back before you even have a chance to miss me."

Jamila did not push the issue any further. As usual, she deferred to Kamil's decision. But in her heart she had already started to miss him.

After a day of hurried preparations for the trip, Kamil set sail for Trabzon. Ten days later the ship's captain brought back news that Kamil Bey had arrived safely in Trabzon.

While Kamil was away, Jamila took the opportunity to spend several weeks with her own parents in Kanlıca. It was the first time she had made an extended visit to them since she married. She had hoped that being with her parents would somehow make the time pass more quickly.

Aware of their daughter's sadness at being separated from Kamil, Hikmet Efendi and Safiye Hanım did their best to keep Jamila busy and occupied. They arranged visits to relatives and neighbors, went on picnics and outings, and they even took Jamila on a nighttime boat tour of the Bosphorus Straits to see the magnificent illuminations made in celebration of the Sultan's birthday. All of the shore houses, gardens and parks were lit up brilliantly by candles fitted in small lanterns in honor of this occasion. The reflection of the illuminations on the water of the straits enchanted Jamila, until she remembered that Kamil was far away ministering to cholera patients. She wished that he had been at her side to share these magical moments.

After spending a month with her parents, Jamila wanted to return to her Beylerbeyi home just in case Kamil returned early. At the end of each day she put an X on the calendar date, feeling that she was one day closer to her reunion with Kamil.

Six weeks passed, eight weeks passed, but still there was no news from Kamil. It seemed as if time had come to a halt for

Jamila. Days dragged by. Each day began with the hope that that day might see Kamil's return, but then ended in the evening with disappointment.

A full three months had elapsed since Kamil had set out for Trabzon. Why hadn't he returned by now? Jamila became very distraught and anxious. Having lost her appetite, she also began to lose weight.

Fearing for Jamila's health, Osman Efendi decided to send his nephew Ahmet to Trabzon to inquire after Kamil. Two weeks later when Ahmet returned, he had no news regarding Kamil. All he could tell Osman Efendi was that the cholera had spread and that Trabzon was under full quarantine. No ships were allowed to enter or depart from the Trabzon port.

This news only served to increase Jamila's anxiety. Kamil's parents had become very concerned about their son's safety as well. Not knowing what action to take under these circumstances, Osman Efendi decided to call upon the Chief Physician at the palace to see if he had any information regarding Kamil.

Upon close questioning, Osman Efendi learned that Kamil had also contracted cholera. However, the Chief Physician had no details about Kamil's condition. An official delegation had been sent to the region to make a report on the dimensions of the disease. The delegation was expected back within several weeks, at which time Osman Efendi would be able to learn more about his son's condition. The Chief Physician assured Osman Efendi that he would inform him as soon as he learned anything further regarding Kamil.

Osman Efendi returned home with a heavy heart. He was reluctant to inform Seniha Hanım and Jamila about Kamil's condition, but they understood that something was wrong as soon as they saw his face.

"Osman Efendi," said Seniha Hanım with a troubled look on her face, "what has happened to Kamil?"

"Well...I couldn't learn much," stammered Osman Efendi.

"For God's sake, tell us everything you know," entreated Seniha Hanım.

Jamila's face turned pale and she held her breath in anticipation of his answer.

Realizing that not saying anything might lead his wife and Jamila to think the worst, Osman Efendi told them exactly what he had learned from the Chief Physician.

Jamila was devastated. Even the thought of losing Kamil overwhelmed her. He was the center of her life, and all her thoughts and actions revolved around him.

The following days and weeks creeped by at a snail's pace. Time weighed heavily on Jamila's heart. She tried to keep herself busy, but she was unable to concentrate on anything else. Inevitably she found herself sitting in front of the large bay window in the couple's sitting room, looking out at the straits, praying for Kamil's recovery.

A full three weeks after Osman Efendi's conversation with the Head Physician at the Palace, a messenger from the royal palace informed Osman Efendi that the delegation had returned from the Black Sea region and that they would be getting news regarding Kamil the next day.

Jamila was both relieved that news of Kamil was on the way, but anxious at the same time regarding the nature of the news to come. Unable to sleep that night, Jamila tossed and turned in her bed in anticipation of the news that the next day would bring.

Exhausted from a lack of sleep, Jamila was up the next morning at breakfast time as usual. She and Kamil's parents spoke little throughout the meal. Jamila only toyed with her food as her thoughts were fully focused on Kamil. As the three of them sipped their morning coffee, a knock was heard on the front door. Contrary to custom, Osman Efendi himself rushed to the door before any servant could reach there. He wanted to get news of

Kamil firsthand. Seniha Hanım and Jamila waited at the entrance to the harem.

As Osman Efendi opened the main door, his voice resounded throughout the entrance hall:

"My son, thank God you are safe and sound!"

Standing at the threshold of the door, Kamil was gaunt and pale. But he was alive and safe. After kissing his father's right hand, Kamil and his father embraced and then hurriedly walked towards the door of the harem. Hearing the men's voices, Seniha Hanım and Jamila both had tears of joy in their eyes. Kamil embraced his mother warmly and then turned towards Jamila. As their eyes met, Jamila silently thanked God in her heart. The trial of separation was over. It had taken its toll, but they had both endured. Now it was the precious time of reunion.

Before long Jamila and Kamil had both fully regained their health. Their trial of separation had made their bonds grow even stronger, and Jamila exulted in the warmth and safety of Kamil's love. Her marital bliss was crowned when she learned two years into her marriage that she was expecting a baby. As an expectant mother, Jamila was both elated and humbled by the divine trust that had been given to her. She felt herself to be an active agent in the sacred process of creation, and she took her responsibility very seriously. She spent many hours in solitude in her favorite spot in front of the windows overlooking the straits. While contemplating the majesty and beauty of God reflected in nature, she talked to her baby and envisioned its spirit to be full of love and light. All of her thoughts and emotions were directed towards enhancing her baby's mind and spirit.

As Jamila's delivery date drew near, preparations for the baby's arrival intensified. The room next to the suite of Jamila and Kamil was furnished appropriately as a nursery. For the first time a European washstand was introduced into the mansion to facilitate the baby's needs. Seniha Hanım had a beautiful cradle carved from wood inlaid with mother-of-pearl. Special sheets, covers and swaddling clothes were all prepared well in advance.

When labor pains began, a trusted midwife was called in. Seniha Hanım, Safiye Hanım and Gulshah Dadı, as well as several kalfas, were all present to help Jamila through the birth. The women supported and comforted Jamila through close to fourteen hours of contractions. The midwife helped Jamila to sit in a special birthing chair that Seniha Hanım had used during Kamil's birth. It had a high back and side arms for the mother's support, and the seat of the chair had been scooped out. Once Jamila sat in the chair, the birth progressed rapidly, and a new baby boy was born amidst exclamations of "God is great" by the women.

The midwife cut the umbilical cord, washed the baby in warm water, wrapped him up and gave him to his mother. Jamila thought he looked like a little prince. After the mother and baby rested a while, Kamil was called into the room to see his new son. Taking the bundle into his arms, he chanted the call to prayer in the child's right ear and pronounced his new name: Ziya. Before the birth Jamila and Kamil had decided to call the baby Ziya (meaning light) if it was a boy or Nur (light) if it was a girl.

Turning to his wife, Kamil asked, "Jamila, are you alright?"

"I'm fine, just a little tired," replied Jamila, with a smile of contentment on her face.

Looking at the baby boy, Kamil said, "Thank you for bringing Ziya into our lives. He's a strong, beautiful baby."

"God willing, he'll grow up to be an admirable man like his father," added Jamila.

A male servant was dispatched to give the good news to neighbors and relatives, and to inform the women that Jamila would be receiving visitors two days later.

On the third day Jamila's female friends, neighbors and relatives all came to see her and the baby and to give their congratulations. Many of them brought small gold charms which were attached to the cradle cushion. All brought gifts according to their means. Some of the women had knitted sweaters and caps for the newborn. It was a very festive occasion. Jamila's bed was decorated with a bower of costly shawls tied together with scarves. The silk bed covers were richly embroidered and decorated with precious stones, as were the cradle covers.

Lying on the bed, Jamila was elegantly dressed in a deep purple caftan with a white satin *shalvar* and white silk blouse underneath. She wore a necklace of three strands of large pearls with an oval diamond clasp holding them together in the middle, which her in-laws had just given her as a gift in appreciation for their new grandchild. Her hair was made into a braided twist attached to the top of her head with diamond hair pins and gold-colored gauze.

There was a great commotion in the room. In one corner several young slave girls were singing and keeping beat to the music with tambourines in their hands. Other slave girls were busy serving the guests a special spicy sherbet made only at births. It was a joyful celebration. The women guests were laughing and talking with Jamila and visiting with one another. Amazingly enough, little Ziya was sound asleep at his mother's side, having nursed to his heart's content. Before the women left, they were all invited to a *mevlut,* * a religious celebration to be held on the seventh day after Ziya's birth.

On the fortieth day after the birth, there was another festive event to celebrate the end of confinement for mother and child. Until that day neither had ever been left alone. This event was the fortieth day bath for the mother and baby. To accommodate the many guests, it was decided to hold the celebration in the public bath. Early in the morning the midwife joined Jamila, Ziya, Seniha Hanım, Safiye Hanım, Gulshah Dadı and many friends

---

* A religious ceremony during which a poem commemorating the birth of the Prophet Muhammad is recited along with hymns and verses of the Quran.

and relatives at the local public bath house. While the guests were being entertained by gypsy music and dance and served sweets and coffee, Jamila and the baby were busy inside the bathing rooms. Gulshah Dadı applied a concoction of aromatic honey all over Jamila's body to restore vigor and vitality. The honey was left on for an hour before it was washed off. Meanwhile, the midwife applied fresh duck egg to the baby's body and then recited some special prayers as she washed away the egg. The entertainment continued throughout the day, and climaxed with a banquet in the afternoon.

Ziya was an easy baby to care for. After several months of adjustment to his new world, baby Ziya began sleeping soundly all night long. Calm and content, he made very few demands on his mother and those around him. Gulshah Dadı insisted on being his nursemaid, and Jamila joyfully accepted. Even though he was the center of attention for two loving parents and four doting grandparents, Ziya did not become a spoiled child. His naturally sweet disposition attracted everyone's attention and affection, but the love and care he received only seemed to nourish his sweetness rather than spoil it.

When Kamil was away, Jamila devoted all her time and energy to Ziya's training and care. He added a profound dimension to her life that was impossible to understand before personally becoming a mother. The bond between a mother and child was truly an extraordinary blessing, and she understood better now why mothers were so revered in Ottoman society.

Important events in Ziya's early childhood were always celebrated with family and friends: his first tooth, his first *hatim,* * his first day of school, his circumcision. When Ziya was four years, four months and four days old, his maternal grandfather Hikmet Bey began to teach him to read the Quran. It was believed that this was the age when a child could first distinguish between right and

---

* Reading the Quran from beginning to end.

wrong. Jamila had a richly embroidered Quran cover prepared, and every morning Ziya would sit on his knees in front of his mother and have his lesson in Quran reading. Ziya was quick to learn, and when he completed reading the Quran, a large family dinner was given.

A huge celebration was held for Ziya's circumcision when the boy was seven years old. It almost rivaled his parents' wedding. Ten other young neighborhood boys from poor families who couldn't afford private celebrations were circumcised along with Ziya. They were all dressed up in special costumes made just for the occasion and led through the neighborhood on horseback. Beds for the boys were prepared in one of the large rooms in the mansion and the room was decorated in bright colors. Although Kamil made most of the circumcisions for the other boys, a colleague made Ziya's circumcision. The boys were all generously given gifts of clothing and gold coins, and they were entertained with clowns and music. Adults were hosted for three days with feasting and music in the *selamlık* and the harem. All the boys remained for a week in the mansion until they recuperated, after which time they returned to their own homes.

The only sorrow that marred Ziya's childhood years was the loss of his paternal grandparents when he was ten years old. Osman Efendi and Seniha Hanım had embarked on a ship sailing to France to attend a trade fair in Paris. The ship capsized in a sudden storm off the coast of Greece. There were no survivors. The loss of his parents deeply affected Kamil, because he had consulted them on every move he made. Their wisdom and dedication to Kamil's success had enabled him to advance quickly in his career. He had recently been appointed as assistant chief physician to the Sultan. No matter how hard Jamila tried to console her husband, she was unable to disperse his depression. Kamil felt as though he had lost his bearings in life.

Remembering the death of Kamil's parents in the previous year, Jamila said a prayer for them as the carriage approached the mansion of her childhood friend, Rabia. The driver stopped the carriage in front of the main entrance and the women climbed out. A visit to Rabia always lifted Jamila's spirits. They had been close friends since childhood and knew each other inside out. Although Rabia had been married for ten years, she was childless. But she didn't allow this condition to get her down. Instead she spent much of her time helping people less fortunate than herself. She had taken in several orphans and was raising them in her own home. Today she had called friends and neighbors from far and wide to help complete the trousseau of a young local orphan girl who was about to be married. It was Rabia who had arranged the girl's marriage with the son of a silk merchant from Bursa.

As soon as Jamila walked through the door of the mansion, she could hear the bustling activity in the harem upstairs. When she and her kalfas entered the large anteroom, they found close to a hundred women, including the servants, gathered together working on various trousseau items. Some women were cutting dress material while others were busy sewing the pieces together. Several ladies were embroidering different corners of a large quilt cover. Two elderly aunts of Rabia were making lace for the edges of pillowcases. A group of young *cariye*s were embroidering dinner napkins. Rabia was busy cutting a bolt of toweling into individual pieces that were being hemmed and decorated by a group of neighbors. Looking up and seeing her friend, Rabia came to meet Jamila with a big smile on her face, and the two women embraced.

"Jamila, I'm so glad you've come. It wouldn't have been the same without you," Rabia said.

"Actually, Rabia, you're the one who makes the greatest difference. None of us would be here today if it weren't for you," replied Jamila, returning her friend's compliment.

"Come and sit down beside me. Your radiance is enough to inspire us all," prompted Rabia, "even if you don't sew a stitch!"

Jamila and her kalfas sat down next to Rabia and helped embroider the cut toweling in silver and gold thread. Jamila was impressed by the industry and skill with which all the women in the hall were working. Their preoccupation with their work, however, did not prevent them from chatting with each other at the same time. Across the room Jamila saw one of Rabia's cousins, Refia Hanım, who had come all the way from Sarıyer by boat to give a helping hand. It gave Jamila a great sense of satisfaction to see all these women spending their time and effort working together to help someone in need.

After a break around 11:00 o'clock for the morning meal, all the women continued working industriously until mid-afternoon. Many of the trousseau items were finished. A number of Rabia's friends planned to spend the night to complete the remaining items. Jamila excused herself because she needed to be home in time for dinner with Kamil and Ziya, but she left one of her kalfas behind to help.

On her way home Jamila counted her blessings. She felt so fortunate to have her parents, Kamil, Ziya, Gulshah Dadı and wonderful friends like Rabia. She knew that but for God's grace, she might have been in the shoes of those less fortunate than herself. It was this knowledge that made Jamila humble, grateful and kind.

CHAPTER 5

Dolmabahce Palace, 1867

A buzz of excitement ran throughout the palace. It was the eve of the first day of the holy month of Ramadan, which everyone would observe by fasting from just before dawn to sunset. The whole palace had been cleaned from top to bottom in anticipation of this special time. Didenur and Servetseza were sitting with Aliye Sultan in her suite after she had finished eating dinner. The princess had twenty-two slave women in her service, but she felt closest to Didenur and Servetseza. The two girls, now sixteen and seventeen years-old, had both become beautiful young women, but Servetseza was stunning. She stood out even in a palace full of beautiful women. They had moved to a room directly under the princess' apartment a year ago when Aliye Sultan lost her mother to tuberculosis. After Tiryal Hanım Efendi's death, Aliye Sultan grew even closer to her two companions. Now sixteen, she had been engaged to a *pasha* by her father, the Sultan, and was to be married shortly after the Ramadan holiday.

"Let's hurry and go. We don't want to be late for the *teravih** prayer," urged Aliye Sultan.

"We still have half an hour, my Sultan," replied Servetseza.

---

* A special ritual prayer made together with the nighttime prayer only during the month of Ramadan.

"You seem to have forgotten how embarrassing it was when the three of us were late last Ramadan, my beautiful sister. Princesses are expected to be perfect. They are never supposed to be late!" exclaimed Aliye Sultan with mock indignation.

Didenur responded smiling at Servetseza, "Aliye Sultan is right, Servetseza. Besides, since princesses are perfect, you know who will be to blame if we're late!"

The three girls got up and made their ablutions before going to the largest hall in the imperial harem where all the women were to make the *teravih* prayer together. When they arrived at the hall, many women were already there, sitting quietly making *zikir* with their prayer beads. Aliye Sultan proceeded to the front of the hall which was reserved for the royal women, and Servetseza and Didenur took their places among the other *cariye*s. Shortly thereafter, the religion teacher highest in rank began to pray and everyone followed suit. The night prayer and the *teravih* prayer together took more than an hour. Several slave women who had memorized the Quran recited long verses at the end of the prayer. Everyone wished each other a wonderful Ramadan and then the women all dispersed.

Didenur and Servetseza made up their beds, undressed and went to sleep as soon as they got back to their room, because they would be getting up around three o'clock in the morning to have a meal before the next day's fast began. The whole palace would follow this schedule throughout the month of Ramadan.

At three in the morning Didenur awoke to the smell of freshly baked flat bread. She got up and went into the next room to find that the pantry service had already set up the *sahur* *trays with olives, cheese, sausage and various jams. There were also egg dishes and freshly made pastry with a minced meat filling. Except for those serving the princess, the kalfas and other girls in Aliye Sultan's service sat down together and made their first Ramadan

* Meal eaten before dawn during the month of Ramadan.

meal. Although Didenur was not particularly hungry at this early hour, she knew she would be by the time of the next meal at sunset.* After everyone had eaten their fill, the *cariye*s spent their time in worship – praying, reading the Quran and making *zikir* with their prayer beads. A short while after the morning prayer, they all went back to sleep.

Around eight o'clock Didenur and Servetseza got up and dressed. They had to go to the sewing room to have their measurements taken. New dresses were to be made before the *Eid* of Ramadan** for all the women in the imperial harem – both royal women and slave women. In the afternoon they had been invited to accompany Aliye Sultan to the large hall located between the harem and the palace offices, where a religious scholar was going to give a special Ramadan lesson and a *hafiz* was going to recite portions of the Quran. The royal women could listen to these men secluded behind screens and grills.

When Didenur, Servetseza and Aliye Sultan arrived at the hall, most of the royal women were already seated there. Aliye Sultan took her place among them, while Didenur and Servetseza sat on cushions in the back of the room. Although Didenur could not see any of the men from her position, she knew that it was custom for the Sultan and his ministers to attend these lessons, as well. Shortly, the arrival of the Sultan was announced and everyone stood up and bowed. Ten minutes later the theologian began to speak about fasting and its benefits. He particularly dwelled on the importance of disciplining one's ego by denying things that are normally lawful to it. After he spoke for forty-five minutes, the *hafiz* began to recite the Quran. Didenur was deeply touched by the power and beauty of the chanting. She didn't know why,

---

* Since there is fasting all day long during Ramadan, usually only two meals a day are eaten: the *sahur* before sunrise and the *iftar* at sunset.

** A 3 day holiday celebrated at the end of the month of Ramadan when fasting finishes.

but it brought tears to her eyes. She looked at Servetseza's face and saw tears streaming down her friend's cheeks as well. After half an hour of recitation, the program was concluded with a long prayer made by the theologian.

As soon as the Sultan and his ministers left, the women dispersed as well. They all went back to their rooms to await the boom of the cannon that would announce the end of the fast. Didenur was feeling a little light-headed, but she knew her body would get accustomed to fasting in 2-3 days, as it always had over the years when she fasted. A half hour before sunset the girls in the pantry service came in and set up the dinner trays. The girls in the food service followed close behind. Didenur and the other girls took their places at the dinner trays to await the cannon boom. Fasting always made the young Circassian girl more grateful for the blessing of food. As soon as the cannon fired, everyone broke their fast with dates sent to the palace from the Hijaz. After eating a few appetizers, the girls made the evening prayer and then sat down to enjoy the rest of the meal. Soup, meat and vegetable dishes and rice were topped off with a special Ramadan dessert made from thin layers of starch wafers, walnuts, rose water and sweetened milk.

Ramadan evenings in the palace were always entertaining. Sometimes princesses who lived outside the palace came to visit their sisters, or former slave women who had gained their freedom and set up their own households would also come back to visit. On some evenings the *cariye*s just visited among themselves. Often the senior kalfas would tell long stories to entertain the younger girls. This evening Aliye Sultan invited Didenur and Servetseza to join her, because she did not have much time remaining before she would leave the palace to set up her own establishment.

"My dear sisters," remarked Aliye Sultan, "I learned today that I'll be living in Vanikoy until the construction of my own palace is completed. You will come and visit me there, won't you?"

"Of course, we will," replied Didenur. "We'll miss you dearly."

"Servetseza, your term of service is finishing. Will you stay in the palace or marry and leave like me?" asked the princess.

"I hope to leave and have my own household, my sultan, but I haven't requested it yet," replied the Georgian beauty.

"How about you, Didenur? Will you be leaving as well?" Aliye Sultan asked.

"I haven't decided yet, my sultan. Ferahshad Kalfa asked me to stay, but I have to think about it some more," responded Didenur.

This subject had been preoccupying Didenur's thoughts for some time. Her nine years of mandatory service were about to end. She had been asked to remain as a permanent member of the palace staff. In time she would most likely be promoted to the rank of junior kalfa and then eventually senior kalfa. She could even aspire to the highest positions in the imperial harem like the posts of Harem Stewardess or Harem Treasurer. These positions carried great responsibility and prestige. The Harem Stewardess was the only person besides the Sultan and Grand Vizier who was entitled to carry the imperial seal. This high office was generously recompensed and the Stewardess had her own staff, which consisted of several senior kalfas and twenty junior kalfas. Moreover, she had the means to build monumental public works. The current Harem Stewardess had built a mosque, a fountain and a public bath. When these women retired from their posts, they lived in a building next to the imperial harem and were well taken care of for life. It was a safe career path to follow.

On the other hand, however, there was Didenur's strong desire to have her own family. She dearly loved children and wanted very much to have her own. As a *saraylı* she could expect to be married into the Ottoman ruling elite. Palace girls were usually given in marriage to men who had been former palace slaves, but who had risen to prestigious positions in the Ottoman military or bureaucracy. Furthermore, upon her emancipation and marriage, the Sultan gave each palace girl a house, furnishings, a trousseau and a pension for life. Any time she was in need, she could rely on the royal family for support, and her connection to the palace carried great weight in society. Didenur was carefully considering both roads open to her, but she didn't want to make a final decision until after Aliye Sultan's wedding. She wanted to give all her time and energy to this marvelous princess who had always treated her with kindness and consideration.

The two young girls sat and talked with Aliye Sultan for hours and reminisced about their years together in the palace. They all laughed when Aliye Sultan mentioned the peacock in the palace garden. They remembered the fun they had on the Ramadan holidays when the palace gardens would be turned into an amusement park. Seesaws, merry-go-rounds, and ferris wheels were set up on the palace grounds for the young princes, princesses and *saraylıs* to amuse themselves. Dressed in their holiday best, the girls played to their heart's content. Later on when they grew older, they waited until evening to go out after all the men had left. When the princess mentioned her mother, the girls all got tears in their eyes. Sharing the sorrow of being separated from their mothers, they made a special prayer for Tiryal Hanım Efendi. Since it had grown very late, Aliye Sultan insisted they have the *sahur* meal with her before they went to bed.

The days of fasting sped by and soon, it was the Night of Power, a major religious holiday that was celebrated solemnly by the whole city of Istanbul. That night the Sultan always went to one of the major mosques in the city for the night prayer. Great pomp and ceremony accompanied his passage to the mosque and the royal princesses always went in their individual carriages to view it. Aliye Sultan requested that Didenur and Servetseza accompany her to the ceremony in her carriage.

The whole street leading from the palace to the mosque was decorated and lit up with gas lamps. The carriages of the princesses lined up side-by-side on the esplanade of the Grand Master of Artillery well before sunset to get a good view of the passage of the military parade accompanying the Sultan. Every place was illuminated with colorful lamps, and there were even banners of lights spelling out pious messages strung between the minarets. When the cannon boom announcing the end of the fast was heard, small trays of prepared food were brought to the princesses' carriages by the eunuchs. Soon the streets and balconies were full of spectators.

Twenty-one cannon shots announced the approach of the Sultan and his retinue; his entourage slowly advanced towards the mosque, and a series of fireworks followed his passage. Once the Sultan had passed, the carriages of the princesses continued to the mosque. Inside, the royal women and their attendants went to the private, imperial lodge. From there, they participated in the prayers and listened to the sermon and the recitations of the Quran. It was an unforgettable experience for Didenur.

Although there were still a few days of fasting left, everyone's mind began to focus on the upcoming three-day holiday. There was great excitement in the air. Final touches were being put on the new dresses that had been sewn for all the girls and women. In the palace, kitchens a legion of cooks were preparing special holiday foods, especially sweets. Men were busy in the palace grounds setting up the amusement rides. Didenur always felt mixed emotions at the end of the Ramadan fast. On the one hand, she was eager for the holiday celebration to begin, but she also felt a little sad that this sacred time was drawing to an end.

Finally, the morning of the first day of celebration arrived. Didenur and Servetseza went up the private stairs and helped Aliye Sultan dress in her new clothing well before dawn. The girls congratulated the princess on the holiday and, as gifts, Aliye Sultan gave Didenur and Servetseza each a dress from her own wardrobe.

Extending the dresses to the two palace girls, the princess said, "May you wear them in good health and good fortune. I hope you will remember me affectionately when you put these dresses on."

"We will always remember you with love, my sultan, and with gratitude for your kindness and generosity," said Didenur.

"May every thread in these dresses testify to your graciousness and your thoughtfulness, my sultan," added Servetseza.

Then Aliye Sultan left with the other young royal princesses and consorts to attend the great parade of the Sultan's passage to the mosque for the holiday prayer. It was a magnificent ceremony with the Sultan and his entourage passing on horseback through an avenue lined on both sides by cavalry troops. The people watched the parade from behind the troops. Leading the parade, the ministers in dress uniform were followed by the Grand Vizier and the *Shayhulislam.* * The Sultan followed at a distance on a white horse with rich trappings. All along the way, a bugle sounded three times as the Sultan approached, and the troops shouted in perfect unison: "Long live my Sultan!" It was a spectacular ceremony with tens of thousands in attendance.

After the parade, the princesses and consorts returned to the palace, and the other married princesses who lived outside the palace began to arrive. They were all escorted to private rooms where they rested and were served coffee and sweets. Then, at the appointed time, the princesses and their attendants went to a gallery running around three-fourths of the Grand Hall where the Sultan would accept congratulations from all the Ottoman dignitaries and foreign ambassadors. There was a grill on the gallery so that the women could see the activities in the hall without being seen.

The Sultan was seated on a magnificent throne. All of the princes in dress uniform stood on his right and the ministers stood on his left. Taking their place according to protocol, the guests approached one by one, made a deep bow and then kissed one end of a large red velvet band decorated with gold that was held by a palace dignitary. The other end of the band was attached to the throne. Music played by the imperial orchestra accompanied

---

* Chief religious official in the empire.

this lengthy ceremony. After it was completed, the Sultan came to receive congratulations in the imperial harem.

Waiting for the Sultan's approach, the harem band of approximately eighty young *cariye*s, dressed in red velvet *shalvar*s and tunics trimmed in gold thread, stood in rapt attention. The Chief Treasurer announced the approach of the Sultan, who was followed by the female servants in his personal service. The band began to play the Imperial March, and the Valide Sultan took her place at the right of the Sultan. Approaching the Sultan one-by-one according to age, the princesses held their hands crossed on their chests in a position of respect. They made a deep bow and then took their place to the right of the Sultan. Similarly, the consorts of the Sultan approached, bowed and took their place on his left. Then two young girls brought in a large napkin embroidered in gold, which contained hundreds of brand new gold coins. The Chief Treasurer tossed these coins by the handfuls to the *cariye*s. One of the coins rolled close to Didenur and she quickly bent down and picked it up.

The *cariye*s all paid their respects to the Sultan. When Didenur and Servetseza approached him, the Sultan indicated that he wanted to have a few words with Servetseza. He had asked this beautiful slave girl to become his consort on several occasions, but she refused him each time.

"Servetseza, you look breathtaking today as always. I hope you are not persisting in your stubbornness. Won't you reconsider my offer?" asked the Sultan.

"My Lord, as long as I am alive, I will be ready to sacrifice my life for you. I will not desert you. But if you grant me the whole world, I will not become your concubine. The man who will become my husband must have only one wife; that is, I wish him to belong to only me. Otherwise I will not marry anyone," replied the beautiful *cariye*.

Looking disappointedly at Servetseza, the Sultan said, "As you wish."

She and Didenur moved on, exchanging holiday congratulations with other women in the hall. Didenur greatly admired Servetseza's courage. Not many of the young palace women would have foregone the privileges of being a consort to the Sultan; in fact, most of them would have been honored. But Servetseza's character was cut from a different cloth. She knew what she wanted from life, and she was determined to get it. She simply refused to accept the unacceptable regardless of how enticing the wrapper was.

The girls spent the holidays socializing with the other women in the palace. There were plays and music in the courtyard which the older girls watched from behind windows with grills, and again there were amusement rides for the little *cariye*s. On the day after the celebrations the equipment was all dismantled and the court was swept clean and restored to its former condition.

After the holidays Servetseza was informed by the Harem Stewardess that the Sultan had arranged a marriage for her with a palace diplomat. She was to be married one month later, and she would be given a furnished house and trousseau, including jewels, a gold watch, a silver coffee set and a set of ivory spoons. She would also receive a small pension from the royal treasury. In addition, everyone in the palace, from the most inexperienced young slave to the Sultan himself, received a daily stipend. Servetseza had saved this money from the time she entered the palace, as did the other girls. Each month she turned over her stipend to one of the retired *cariye*s living next to the imperial harem, who kept the accumulated money in a small chest with Servetseza's name on it. The money would be turned over to her upon leaving the palace.

Didenur was extremely happy for Servetseza, but a little sad at the same time. The girls had been like sisters throughout their days in the palace, and they had grown into adulthood together. They had shared everything -their problems, their dreams, their joys. Servetseza promised she would come back to the palace to visit Didenur as long as she was there, but it would never be the same again.

Meanwhile, preparations for Aliye Sultan's wedding were continuing at full speed. Her fiancée, Ahmet Pasha, had sent her a brilliant, large diamond ring and earrings to match. In addition, there were many silver trays holding various perfumes, bowls of musk, crystal carafes of syrup, porcelain vases of preserves and Chinese porcelain plates full of fruits and candies. The royal princess shared the fruit and candy with all the girls in her service. She also gave Didenur and Servetseza several bottles of the perfume. The royal palace sent reciprocal gifts to the bridegroom.

Aliye Sultan's trousseau had been ordered well in advance. Jewelry, silverware and gold and silver embroideries were being prepared by reputable Armenian jewelers in the Covered Bazaar. The chief jeweler had brought samples of jewelry and silverware to the imperial harem for the Valide Sultan to see. After she chose the desired items, the Head of the Harem Treasury carefully placed the order. A skilled seamstress had been called into the palace to prepare the princess' dresses.

The Sultan commanded that the official marriage be held at the palace of the *Shayhulislam*. The top eunuchs of the imperial harem acted as representative and witnesses for the royal princess, and the Grand Vizier represented the groom. The event was celebrated among men at the *Shayhulislam's* residence.

When the trousseau and wedding gifts were completed, Didenur and Servetseza helped to display them in one of the large halls in the harem. Along with other *cariyes* in Princess Aliye's service, they spread red cloths over three sofas and arranged the items here on trays covered with gauze and ribbons. Among the gifts were: a diamond crown, diamond and pearl necklaces and earrings, several brooches, a belt buckle, a writing set adorned with precious stones, a Quran with a gold cover, a coffee service with saucers encrusted with jewels, spoons with jeweled handles, silverware, porcelain plates, basins with ewers, carafes, goblets and hand mirrors. Ten new silk dresses had been prepared for the trousseau, but the princess' personal wardrobe was not put on display. First the Sultan visited the trousseau display, followed by the imperial harem and then by all the other palace women and girls.

These items, except for the jewelry Aliye Sultan was to wear, were taken across the straits to the bridal home in Vanikoy by royal caiques. The heavier trunks, linens and furnishings were sent by barges covered with red cloth. The officers of the palace and many of the senior kalfas from the personal staffs of the Sultan, the Valide Sultan and the princess went to the seaside bridal mansion to oversee wedding preparations.

On Wednesday evening, the night before the wedding day, a huge celebration was held in the imperial harem among the women. All of the royal women including the Valide Sultan and the princesses living outside the imperial palace were present. A chamber orchestra and dancers provided entertainment for everyone. The young palace girls and women were all dressed elegantly. This was their time to celebrate since among the *cariye*s only the senior kalfas and the women and girls in Aliye Sultan's private service would be able to attend her wedding. Aliye Sultan looked radiant in a pale blue silk dress in a European cut, decorated with lace of the same color. The other royal women were dressed splendidly as well and were adorned with their finest jewelry. Around 10.00 p.m. Aliye Sultan and the other royal women retired, and the *cariye*s shortly followed suit.

The next morning Didenur and Servetseza put on the dresses Aliye Sultan had given them on the Ramadan holiday. They immediately went upstairs to attend the royal princess. Having just finished her breakfast, Aliye Sultan was about to get dressed. All of the girls and women in her service were there to assist her. The bridal dress was champagne white embroidered with gold thread and ornamented with precious jewels. Since a child, the royal princess had worn Western-style clothing, so it was only natural for her to choose a Western-style wedding dress. Her costume was topped off with her diamond crown, diamond necklace and earrings, gold watch, brooch and bracelets of precious stones and several rings, including her wedding ring.

A piece of red cloth was spread all the way down the stairs from the second floor of the palace to the dock where the princess would depart by boat for her new home. The harem orchestra was playing on the first floor and all the palace women had assembled to see her off. Those who would accompany her had put on their outer garments of pastel-colored silk *ferace*s and their veils. Aliye Sultan was accompanied by the most senior official female in the palace and her governess, whom her father had appointed at her birth. Didenur, Servetseza and three other women from the princess' service followed, carrying the long train of her dress. Outside the palace a military band was playing and the black eunuchs were lined up in two rows all the way to the dock. On both sides they held up a continuous piece of red material, thus forming a corridor through which the princess could pass so that she was not seen by the many male palace officials waiting near the dock.

Aliye Sultan boarded the royal ceremonial caique that awaited her. The boat had fourteen pairs of oars and a kiosk furnished with red silk seats trimmed in gold fringe that held eight people. Aliye Sultan sat in the seat that was usually reserved for her father, the Sultan. As soon as Didenur, Servetseza and the other women were all seated, the curtains of the kiosk were closed tight. The oarsmen were dressed in red *shalvar*s and red vests embroidered in gold. They also wore white shirts and red fezs. Two captains dressed similarly in green stood at the rudder, and the chief eunuch and another aide-de-camp, dressed in uniforms and white gloves with swords hanging at their sides, stood just behind the kiosk with their hands folded over their chests in respect. Other smaller boats carrying more royal women and palace officials accompanied the ceremonial caique in a colorful procession with imperial flags flying in the breeze. Hundreds of private boats on the Bosphorus ere held at bay by naval cutters manned by sailors in white uniforms and officers in gold braid.

Arriving at the wharf of the seaside mansion, Aliye Sultan waited for some time in the imperial caique until all the other boats had arrived. The groom, Ahmet Pasha, stood on the dock next to the royal caique and waited for the princess to descend. It was the custom for royal princesses to make their husbands, who were lower in rank, to wait a little. When Aliye Sultan disembarked from the boat, she was escorted by her husband holding her right arm and the chief eunuch holding her left arm. Again Didenur, Servetseza and three other cariyes from the princess's service held the train of her gown as they walked on red felt material extending to inside the mansion through a corridor of red broadcloth stretched along the route. The Imperial March was being played as the princess approached.

Once inside, the couple was led to a large hall where Aliye Sultan's bridal throne had been arranged. After a few brief moments together, the groom was led to the *selamlık* to host the male guests. As was custom, two young girls brought in a napkin of gold coins, which were thrown by the handfuls to the female guests by the Chief Treasurer of the imperial harem. Didenur and Servetseza watched as the princess accepted first her mother-in-law and then the other royal princesses. After them, the wives of the ministers and the Grand Vizier gave their congratulations to the new bride.

When this ceremony was completed, everyone went for the wedding feast. The princesses were fed in individual rooms of the mansion, while the wives of great dignitaries were accommodated two or three to a room. The rest of the women ate at common tables set up in large halls. In the evening after the groom went to the bridal chamber, the women guests were entertained in the harem with singing and dancing while the men were entertained in the *selamlık*. After the festivities, the highest dignitaries and their wives remained for the night, while most of the other guests left. Didenur, Servetseza and the other women in Aliye Sultan's service stayed over to witness the completion of the wedding ceremonies to be held the following day.

On the next day the Sultan and the Valide Sultan came to the wedding celebration. The Sultan first visited Aliye Sultan in her bridal chamber and then he went to the great hall where the women guests were all assembled. The princesses were lined up separately on one wall of the room. The Sultan stood near the princesses and each was presented to him by the Chief Harem Treasurer. After bowing to their father, the princesses lined up next to the queen mother on his right. The other women, beginning with Aliye Sultan's mother-in-law, were presented to the Sultan, and they lined up on the Sultan's left after they had bowed in respect. When this ceremony was complete, the Sultan retired to the *selamlık*. The women guests congratulated the Valide Sultan and then left, bringing the official wedding reception to a close.

The guests all boarded small boats and returned to their homes. After receiving generous purses of money from their princess, Didenur and Servetseza returned to the palace along with other *cariye*s. It had been an extraordinary and emotion-laden experience for them.

"Servetseza, one chapter of our princess's life is closing and a new one is opening. May it be full of good fortune," said Didenur with a tone of both sadness and uncertainty in her voice.

Until now the palace had been a safe and comforting world for Didenur. The presence of Aliye Sultan and Servetseza had made the young Circassian girl's life both purposeful and joyful. But now one of the main sources of her well-being had married and moved on to begin a new stage in life. Shortly, Servetseza would be marrying and leaving the palace, as well. Uncertain about what the future held for her, Didenur felt an unfamiliar anxiety.

Sensing her friend's uneasiness, Servetseza tried to comfort Didenur: "It's true that our princess has closed one chapter in her life. But there always has to be an ending before there can be a new beginning. And who knows, maybe the new stage in her life will be immeasurably better than the last. We all have to grow, Didenur. We have to move on in life. If a caterpillar stays too long in its cocoon, it will die and never have the chance to become a butterfly."

Didenur understood what Servetseza was saying. Sometimes we have to let go in life, but it is difficult to let go of someone you are very close to, even if it is best for them. On the other hand, Aliye Sultan would now have her own court and palace. She was no longer one of the young palace princesses. Both her position and her duties had increased greatly by marrying. Irrevocably entering the adult world, the princess would carry a much graver responsibility from now on. But Didenur knew that Aliye Sultan had been well prepared for her new role and that she welcomed it. She knew the princess would become a beautiful "butterfly."

Back at the palace everyone was curious about the wedding and Aliye Sultan's new home. The evening was spent describing the wedding celebration to many of the *cariye*s who had been unable to attend. They wanted to know all the details about the wedding, the bride and groom, and their new residence. Even though they were both exhausted, Didenur and Servetseza spent hours talking with other girls, giving their eyewitness account of the princess's wedding celebration.

Immediately after Aliye Sultan's wedding, the women and girls from her service were given new assignments. Servetseza would shortly be going to the home of a freed, married *saraylı* living outside the palace until her own marriage took place. Didenur was assigned to the service of Juret Hanım, the Sultan's latest concubine. Although this royal consort was an attractive Circassian girl, she had a very bold personality that rubbed Didenur the wrong way. A combination of ambition and over self-confidence made Juret Hanım demanding and haughty, and she did not hesitate to voice her disapproval when she was displeased.

"Didenur, I expect your full attention to my services," said the royal consort in a harsh tone of voice. "I'll accept no laziness on the part of my attendants."

"Yes, my lady," Didenur replied politely, but she was stung by the sharp remark. In the nine years that Didenur had been in Aliye Sultan's service, the princess had never spoken to her in a harsh manner. Had Juret Hanım forgotten so quickly that until recently she had just been a slave girl in the service of the Valide Sultan? In addition, Didenur was known and admired throughout the palace for her diligence and thoroughness. Had not the Chief Kalfa personally asked her to stay on at the imperial harem? How could this new royal consort even suggest that she might be lazy?

Didenur knew that Juret Hanım was unpopular among the palace girls, and now she began to see why. Was it just the girl's natural make-up or had her head been turned by the prestige of her new position? Or both? The strict etiquette enforced in the palace was usually enough to smooth over the rough edges in individual personalities. But apparently the Sultan's sudden attention had made Juret Hanım feel powerful enough to disregard palace etiquette. Didenur knew that over the long run, the royal consort would have to conform for her own good, but in the meantime, Didenur would have her hands full if she stayed on at the palace in this young woman's service.

That evening Didenur and Servetseza said their final goodbyes. The next morning Servetseza would be leaving the palace. Of course, they could occasionally see each other in the future, but the intimacy of living together on a daily basis and sharing every detail of their lives was drawing to an end. Didenur tried to focus on her best friend's future rather than on how much she would miss her.

"Servetseza, now you are the one closing one chapter in life and opening another," said Didenur. "How do you feel about it?"

"I feel that everything is just as it should be, Didenur. Yes, I have spent a little more than nine years of my life as a slave girl in the palace. But it has been an amazing education. I don't mean just learning the language and embroidery or other things like that, but, you know, the discipline and principles, the refined manners, the respect and consideration for others. We have had the best training of any women in the Empire, maybe even in the world. Now we have a fantastic network of powerful and caring women to rely on when we need them, not to mention the Sultan, himself. I have a house of my own, an income for life, valuable jewels and clothing and a new husband who has also been trained in the subtleties of the palace. Tomorrow morning I will be given my document of emancipation, and I will have the same status as other Ottoman women. In fact, I have the advantage of being close to the royal family. What more could I ask for, Didenur?"

"Servetseza, I love the way you can pragmatically cut to the heart of the matter and see life in its pristine truth. This gift should serve you well in life."

"And I love the way you have always restrained my impetuosity, Didenur. If it were not for your stabilizing influence on me, I know my years here would have passed with much greater difficulty. We mustn't allow our ties to weaken; you can be sure I'll call on you whenever I get myself into trouble!" commented Servetseza with a faint smile on her face.

Turning her head to hide the tears that were brimming in her eyes, Didenur responded: "I wouldn't have it any other way."

One morning several weeks later when Didenur was in Juret Hanım's apartment, her mind was preoccupied with thoughts about her future. Aliye Sultan had married and left the palace. Servetseza had left to be married shortly. Was it Didenur's turn to leave? Servetseza was right; their nine years of service in the palace had been an extraordinary education, but perhaps now it was time for Didenur to open up a new chapter in life, too. As these thoughts were running through Didenur's mind, the vase of flowers she was carrying to a console in Juret Hanım'a apartment slipped from her hands. The vase broke with a crash as it hit the floor and the water splashed out. The wet flowers and broken vase were in a heap on the floor at Didenur's feet.

Hearing the noise, Juret Hanım immediately rushed into the room. Without giving Didenur a chance to apologize, the royal consort began scolding Didenur.

"Look what a mess you've made! One would think that you are a novice who has just arrived at the palace. Have not you learned anything since you came here? How can you be so clumsy?"

Several other *cariye*s in Juret Hanım's service hurried into the room and everyone was staring at Didenur.

Her first impulse was to apologize for the accident, but after hearing the royal consort's angry tirade of criticism, she simply bent down and picked up the pieces of ceramic and the flowers from the floor. Then she politely asked one of the novices to mop up the water and she went downstairs to the servants' quarters.

Didenur sat down on a sofa and took several deep breaths to regain her composure. She suddenly recalled the time Servetseza had broken a beautiful china doll that a Danish princess had given to Aliye Sultan. The doll had been a favorite toy of the Ottoman princess, but she would occasionally allow Didenur and Servetseza to play with it, too. One day, while the three of them were "playing nurse," Servetseza put the china doll on an end table to "examine" it. As she was taking the doll's "temperature," Servetseza bumped the table and the doll rolled off and broke on the floor. Without the slightest sign of anger, Aliye Sultan had said, "Thank God, what broke is just a doll!" Then she turned to Servetseza, who was crying, and just to make her feel better, the little princess said: "Don't cry, my beautiful sister, I didn't like that doll anyway."

Comparing the two events, Didenur felt today's incident was a sign – a sign indicating that it was time for her to move on in life. If she stayed on at the palace, there were only two options open to her. She would either have to accept the unacceptable and bow to Juret Hanım's overbearing personality, or try to struggle against this young woman's capricious nature. But Didenur knew that such a struggle was full of risks. After all, the new consort currently had the Sultan on her side. In addition, the Valide Sultan obviously had been taken in by the young woman and had recommended the *cariye* to her son. Didenur was sure that in the long run Juret Hanım would get her just desserts; she believed in divine justice. She knew that sooner or later the seeds of our actions sprout, in time grow into fruit-bearing trees and eventually return to us in the form of fruit – bitter or sweet - depending on the seeds we plant. But for now, neither of the two options open to her at the palace appealed to Didenur. Her only other option was to ask to be married and leave the palace to start a new life. Didenur made her decision.

CHAPTER 6

Dolmabahce Palace, 1867

As was custom, Didenur prepared a note for the Sultan requesting permission to leave the palace. It was understood that she was hoping to marry. She gave it to the Chief Kalfa who gave it to the Harem Agah, who in turn passed it on to the Sultan. Two weeks later Didenur's nine-year period of service would be complete and she would receive a document to the effect that she was a free woman. At that time, she would go to the home of a freed *saraylı* until a marriage could be arranged for her. The details of her trousseau would be handled by the Harem Agah, who would make the necessary arrangements with the royal treasury.

The next two weeks flew by fast. Didenur avoided face-to-face contact with Juret Hanım as much as possible, and fortunately, no other unpleasant incident occurred between them. Of course, Didenur was sad to leave the palace; she had made many deep bonds with both the younger *cariye*s and a number of the kalfas. Mushfika Kalfa had become a senior kalfa and Ferahshah Kalfa had moved up in the harem hierarchy to the position of Assistant Treasurer. Both these women had shown Didenur strong support and care over the years. Also she was loved and respected by *cariye*s her own age and particularly by those younger than herself, because Didenur was always eager to help them out. If fate had not put Didenur in Juret Hanım's service, thereby giving her a gentle push out the door, she might never have left the palace.

After receiving her document of emancipation, Didenur was sent to the home of Nazikeda Hanım, a *saraylı* living in a mansion overlooking the Golden Horn. Nazikeda Hanım warmly welcomed Didenur into her home. She was a young woman around twenty-two years of age. Both women remembered each other from the time when Nazikeda was still at the imperial harem, but they had not been close because of their age difference. Nazikeda, also a Circassian, had left the palace a few years after Didenur arrived and they had lost touch. After her manumission, Nazikeda was married to a high-ranking naval officer. They had twin daughters, Hatice and Emine, who were three years-old. With her husband away much of the time, Nazikeda's world revolved around her daughters.

While in the palace, Didenur had suppressed her motherly instincts. But now that she had left palace life behind her, Didenur gave full rein to her motherly instincts. The twins' sweetness and innocence fully captured her heart. The girls were exulted with the extra attention and soon had Didenur wrapped around their little fingers. At least one of them was in Didenur's lap -and sometimes both- from the time they woke up in the morning until they fell asleep at night. Didenur poured out love and affection to them, as if to make up for the years she had spent in the palace remote from close contact with small children. When she went to bed at night, she fantasized about marrying and having her own children. Although large families were not the custom in Istanbul, she wanted to have many children - the more, the better.

News regarding Didenur's marriage was not long in coming. On the fourth day of her visit one of the harem agahs brought the message that a marriage had been arranged for Didenur with a colonel in the army by the name of Davud. The official ceremony would take place a week from Thursday with a harem agah attending as representative of the bride. Didenur's trousseau was being prepared by the palace and would be transported to her new home the day before the wedding. No other information was forthcoming from the harem agah.

The palace official had given just enough information to whet the curiosity of the women. After he left, Nazikeda said that a close friend of hers was married to a general in the army who would surely know of the prospective groom. She suggested that she would be happy to pay her friend a visit if Didenur so wished. Didenur was very grateful, and the matter was decided. Nazikeda would call on her friend and Didenur would stay and oversee the care of the twins. Taking two of her young *cariye*s with her, Nazikeda Hanım set out to learn what she could about Didenur's future husband.

While spending the day with the twins, Didenur's mind frequently strayed to the topic of the prospective groom. She wondered, in particular, what kind of father he would be. Would he want children as much as she did? Would he be a kind and loving father? Would he make his family the center of his world as Didenur planned to do? The young woman impatiently awaited the return of Nazikeda Hanım in expectation of some information about the character of her future husband.

Just as the call from the minaret for the late afternoon prayer was being made, the carriage of Nazikeda Hanım pulled up in front of the house. Nazikeda entered her home with a look of satisfaction on her face. She obviously had some important information for Didenur. After inquiring about the twins to her chief kalfa, Nazikeda led Didenur into a private sitting room where they could talk alone.

"Didenur, Fikret Pasha was very helpful and we were able to get a pretty good profile of Colonel Davud."

"I don't know how to thank you for your help," responded Didenur.

"I am more than happy to help out another *saraylı*," replied Nazikeda. "I know you would have done the same thing for me. Coming to Colonel Davud, I learned that he is forty-two years-old and was born in a village close to Mostar. After learning the

Turkish language and customs and the Islamic religion, he entered a military preparatory school and studied there for another eight years. Afterwards, he was sent to the cavalry division and there he rose in the ranks over the years to his present position. He is an officer known for his strict discipline and hard work. He was married until recently when his wife died from pneumonia. There are no children from that marriage, but his elderly mother lives with him in Beyazıt."

Didenur was pleased with Colonel Davud's background and training. Having been educated in a military preparatory school, he was sure to have been schooled in refined Ottoman etiquette and customs. But there was a question mark in Didenur's mind about his family. Why had not there been any children from the first marriage? Could it be that he didn't want children? This was a question that couldn't be answered by even the pasha's wife. Didenur would just have to wait until some time in the future to learn the truth from the Colonel himself.

The days passed quickly and the day of the official marriage ceremony soon arrived. Didenur wore a new silk dress, which had been sent from the palace for her to wear on this occasion; the rest of her trousseau had been taken to her new home. She also wore the pearl necklace and earrings the Valide Sultan had given her upon her discharge from the palace. The only people in attendance beside the groom were the imam, the palace agah, and Nazikeda's husband and another naval officer who were acting as witnesses to the nuptial ceremony.

Didenur and Nazikeda were waiting in an adjacent room, although Didenur had met with the groom shortly before the ceremony. It was an opportunity for her to see the groom and reject this marriage if she found reason to do so. When they met, Didenur got only a general impression of Colonel Davud, because she was too shy to look him directly in the face. He was tall and slender, but well-built. He had a few gray hairs at the temples, and he looked distinguished in his military uniform. Didenur saw nothing about him that repulsed her, so she proceeded with the marriage.

After the brief ceremony, the men dined in the male quarters, and the women dined in the harem. Didenur ate very little because her stomach was a bit jittery. The gravity of the step she was taking had begun to sink in. With the exception of the traumatic events that had torn her from her homeland and brought her to Istanbul, Didenur had lived a happy and fulfilled life. Of course, this was in part, due to Didenur's being at peace with herself. She looked at the world positively and tried to focus on her blessings. Consequently, she got a positive reflection back from the mirror of reality. Her marriage, however, was a step towards an uncertain future. She could only hope and pray that it would be a fortunate one.

Sensing Didenur's apprehension, Nazikeda began to talk about her own fears and anxiety on her wedding night:

"Stepping out of a totally female world into the arms of a strange man is not an easy thing to do. It reminded me a little too much of Russian roulette. But, thank God, my fears were unfounded. My husband turned out to be a very considerate and warm-hearted person. A deep love has grown up between us, and it was further cemented by the birth of our twins. Don't worry, Didenur, I'm sure everything will work out best for you in the long run."

Didenur gave her a grateful smile. Perhaps she was making too much out of her uncertainty. Surely it must be normal for most brides to have the butterflies on their wedding night. Didenur decided to push her fears aside and enjoy herself.

A half an hour later, a young slave girl announced that Colonel Davud was ready to leave. Didenur put on her veil and *ferace* and thanked Nazikeda for all her help and kindness. Nazikeda reassured the new bride that her door was always open and that she would be eager to help in any way she could. The young women embraced and Didenur left to step into the carriage that was waiting at the front door.

Colonel Davud accompanied the carriage mounted on his horse. The carriage slowly moved along the narrow winding streets. Didenur could hear the commotion of the crowds in the street, but she could not see anything outside because of the tightly drawn curtains. After what seemed a very long ride, the carriage came to an abrupt halt. Colonel Davud opened the carriage door and helped Didenur descend. Her eyes scanned the immediate neighborhood. Unlike the spacious view afforded by the position of Nazikeda's home looking out over the Golden Horn, the houses here were built very close together and only faced each other. There were latticed shutters covering all the windows facing the street. Remembering the vast buildings at the palace, Didenur realized it would take her a while to get used to the small houses cramped together on this narrow street.

A middle-aged slave woman opened the door and Didenur followed Colonel Davud into a sitting room stuffed with an eclectic combination of furniture. Running along one side of the room there was an Ottoman sofa with slightly frayed, once-elegant green and gold brocade cushions. On the opposite wall there were chairs in different European styles with red and blue striped upholstery lined up one after another. The third wall held a huge black lacquered Chinese cabinet, while a German rug with a big yellow lion on it hung on the fourth wall.

Didenur felt disoriented and was trying to make some sense out of it all when Davud's mother entered the room. Somehow the elderly woman looked perfectly at home in this room. She, too, was dressed in an eclectic manner. The woman was wearing what must have originally been a caftan, but the collar of which had been scooped out and trimmed in feathers. On her feet she wore typical Turkish slippers, but she had a white cotton European peasant bonnet on her head. Her costume was topped off with an extraordinary amount of jewelry. Each finger had a ring with a different gemstone and sundry necklaces cascaded down her chest.

Extending her hand for the new bride to kiss, she said in a very heavy accent:

"Very lucky, you're very lucky to get a man like my son." Pointing around the room she continued, "You see, you'll want for nothing. You will have a life of luxury and ease. But you must give us a son!"

Amazed by this woman's words, Didenur looked at Davud. He avoided her glance and just stood there with a helpless look on his face. Realizing that her mother-in-law's hand was still hanging in mid-air, Didenur gathered herself and hurriedly kissed the elderly woman's hand. Confused as to how she should respond to her mother-in-law's words, the new bride remained silent.

Saying, "Davud, show your new wife your room," the elderly woman retired to her own quarters.

The colonel turned and headed towards a closed door leading off the harem sitting room, and Didenur followed. When she entered the room, she felt a slight sense of relief. At least this room didn't have any of the garishness of the sitting room. It was simply furnished with an Ottoman sofa at one end. A large built-in closet at the other end held the bedding and some clothing. There was a small table for reading or writing and a large brass brazier. A bookcase filled with books stood in one corner. A door opened from the room to a space as large as a closet called a *gusülhane*. There was just enough room in it for a single person to comfortably take a bath by pouring water from large jugs.

A servant girl knocked on the door, entered and showed Didenur where some of her trousseau had been put in the closet.

"The rest of your belongings have been put in a storage room, Hanım; I'll be happy to show you the way tomorrow," the girl said with a smile on her face. "Do you need anything, Colonel Efendi?*" the girl inquired.

"You can bring us some fruit," Davud replied.

---

* A term of respect for gentlemen also meaning 'master.'

Davud sat down next to Didenur on the sofa.

"I hope you'll be able to amuse yourself when I'm away, Didenur," said the colonel. "Due to my work, I will not be home much because I spend a lot of time training troops in the field."

Getting up and walking towards the bookcase, Davud asked, "Do you like to read?"

Didenur replied that she did, and he chose a few books he thought she might enjoy. When he handed her the books, Didenur tried to make eye contact with him, but the colonel did not look up.

The servant girl returned with some fruit and Didenur began to peel some apples. Putting the sliced apples on a small plate, she handed it to Davud. Again, she tried to make eye contact with him, and this time he returned her glance. But the look in the colonel's eyes made Didenur shiver. There was no life in his eyes; he had a completely blank look. Didenur felt uneasy. She wondered if he was still mourning for his dead wife. She told herself she would have to be patient with him. In time, surely he would adjust to his new life and turn his attention to her.

Davud called in two servant girls to make up the bed. Didenur found her new nightgown among her belongings in the closet, and she got undressed. She shyly slipped into her new pale blue silk gown. With her long, honey-blond hair brushed over her shoulders, Didenur was exquisite. Her beauty was not provocative like Servetseza's beauty; it was more subtle and refined. Her attractiveness was further compounded by the purity of her character and her elegant manners. In all, Didenur was the kind of bride many men can only dream of…

Early the next morning Didenur got up before dawn to make her ablution before the morning prayer. As she poured water over her head, it mingled with the tears streaming down her cheeks. Why had not Davud found her attractive? Had she done something wrong? Why had he been so silent and so emotionally detached?

No compliments… no sweet words… no emotional engagement… Didenur did not understand. Why had he married her?

Didenur finished her bath, dried off and wrapped her damp hair in a towel. After getting fully dressed, she spread her prayer rug on the floor and performed the morning ritual prayer. Didenur sat on the prayer rug for a long time, entreating God to guide her. She felt so disappointed, so confused and so alone … She knew she was in a situation over her head, and there was no one to give her advice. Her only hope was guidance from God.

Didenur felt the need to be alone, so she decided to go find the storage room where the remainder of her trousseau had been put and busy herself with the items sent by the palace. She asked directions from one of the women servants and was told that the storage room was off the hall leading to the *selamlık*. She walked down the long corridor, stopped and tried the door, but it was locked. As she gently tried to push the door, a servant woman ran towards and told her that door was never to be opened. The storage room door was the next one down the hall. Didenur did not understand what all the fuss was about, but she proceeded to the next door and found it opening into a small room containing chests of clothing and other stored items. When Didenur saw the beautiful dresses, the shiny silverware, the elegant coffee set, the handsome Swiss clock and other household pieces the palace had sent on her behalf, she suddenly felt very homesick. She missed the grandeur of the palace and the dignity and refinement of palace life. Had she made a wrong decision? Should she have remained in that noble world? On the verge of tears, Didenur suddenly recalled the caprices of Juret Hanım. No, she did what she had to do; she had taken the only acceptable option. Now she needed to be patient until her path opened up.

After examining her trousseau carefully, Didenur put everything in its place and left the storage room. As she approached her own room, she heard her mother-in-law speaking in a loud voice to Davud inside. She could not understand what was being said because her mother-in-law was speaking in her native Serbian language. But she was talking in a very harsh and emphatic tone. Davud only sheepishly responded, "I promise, Mama, I promise." When Didenur entered the room, they ended the conversation. A servant girl informed them that the morning meal was ready in the sitting room, and they left the room and took their places at the dining tray.

The next ten days passed in a routine fashion until the colonel had to return to active duty. Didenur tried to get to know Davud better, but the door to his inner world was shut tight. Their conversation always remained on the surface; Didenur was unable to penetrate into his innermost thoughts. Davud, on the other hand, did not reveal any emotions; it was as if his heart had turned to stone.

After the Colonel left, the neighborhood women began calling on Didenur to welcome and congratulate her. Davud's mother spent most of her time idly drinking Turkish coffee and smoking a water pipe in her favorite spot on the sofa in front of a bay window. She would sit there for hours looking out the window as if awaiting Davud's return. She had no other interest or focus in life but her son.

At first, Didenur tried to keep herself busy by reading the books Davud had recommended to her. Then several days later, she discovered, much to her delight, a brand new piano in one of the sitting rooms. When she inquired about it, she learned that it had been bought for the colonel's deceased wife, but that the woman's piano lessons had been cut short by her illness. No one else in the household was able to play it.

Didenur had learned to play the piano as a child in the palace. She and Servetseza had always accompanied Princess Aliye to her piano lessons. One day while the princess was practicing, she asked Didenur if she would like to play the piano along with her. Much to everyone's surprise, Didenur was immediately able to play the simple melody the princess had been practicing for days. Recognizing her talent, the teacher informed the head kalfa, and it was decided that Didenur would also have a lesson after each of Aliye Sultan's piano lessons. Over the years, she had become an accomplished pianist. After getting permission from her mother-in-law to play the piano when she wanted, Didenur spent hours each day pouring out her sorrow and hopes in music.

It was not long before Didenur's accomplishment as a pianist spread around the neighborhood. Guests always asked her to play for them when they came to visit. Then requests for lessons started pouring in. All the well-off women in the neighborhood wanted piano lessons for their children. Soon Didenur even began to get requests from women living in surrounding districts. At first she did not want to take any money, but at everyone's insistence she gave in.

There was, however, one exception: the young girl next door who had recently lost her father. Didenur had noticed the keen interest in the girl's eyes whenever she sat down at the keyboard. Calling her to the piano once when they were alone, Didenur realized that the girl had musical talent. Aware that the military pension the family received due to her father's death would not allow for private lessons, Didenur spoke with her mother. She insisted on teaching the young girl how to play without any recompense. The mother finally gave in when she saw her daughter's desire to learn and her musical talent. Didenur's days were filled with playing the piano and teaching her students. This not only made her feel fulfilled that she was doing something worthwhile, but it also helped to stabilize her emotionally.

Her peace of mind was broken only by her mother-in-law's negative attitude. At first the woman had acted amicably enough towards Didenur after Davud had left for duty. But a few weeks later her attitude suddenly turned sour. Didenur was confused as to the reason for it. She carefully examined her own behavior towards Davud's mother, but she could not find any obvious fault. Later Didenur overheard her mother-in-law complaining to the head kalfa about Didenur not being pregnant. This upset the woman very much because she was determined to see a grandson before she died. This conversation suddenly explained the reason for her mother-in-law's negativity towards her and the commanding tone she had used with her son when they were alone together. But what could Didenur do about it? She also wanted a child very badly, but it was not in her hands.

Didenur's mother-in-law never left her position in front of the window except for eating and sleeping. It was as if she was trying to force her son's return by sitting there concentrating on it. Whether it was her success or just coincidence, the Colonel suddenly returned home one evening a month after he had left. At first Didenur was very excited to see him, but the blank look in his eyes reminded her that Davud was not excited to see her. He was polite, but not enthusiastic. After dinner, Davud spoke briefly about his work, and Didenur told him about her students. She played a few pieces on the piano for him, but he did not show much interest, so they retired to their room. After they went to bed, Didenur thought she heard a noise. Could some one be listening at the door?

The next morning again tears streamed down Didenur's face as she made her ablution in the small closet-like bathroom next to her bedroom. She felt totally unfulfilled as a woman. Except on the physical plane, Davud had not been at all engaged in the act of making love. He was not involved with her personally; Didenur felt as if she could have been any other woman and it would not have made any difference for Davud. She was very confused. On the one hand, she dearly wanted to have a baby. Just the sight of a neighborhood child was enough to trigger a deep, motherly yearning inside of her. But on the other hand, Davud's lack of interest in her made Didenur wary of conceiving a child with him. Her instinct told her that the quality of the bond between a man and woman at the moment of conception would somehow have an important impact on the child in some way. Since she wanted only the best for her future children, Didenur wanted to conceive a child out of love. It was more than obvious that Davud felt no love for her, and her initially positive feelings for him were being extinguished by his indifference towards her.

A few days later as Didenur was going down the hall to play the piano, she saw Davud entering the locked room next to the storage room. He took a key out of his pocket, entered the room and locked it from the inside. Didenur became curious and decided to wait in the storage room until Davud left. More than an hour later the colonel left the room and locked it again. Didenur couldn't make any sense out of it. What was he doing in the room, and why all this secrecy?

Two days later as Didenur was again going down the hall to play the piano, she saw that the door to the locked room was open. The servant woman cleaning the room had temporarily left the door unlocked. Didenur seized the opportunity and immediately went inside. As soon as she entered the room, she understood that this was the bedroom belonging to Davud and his former wife. As she looked around the room, Didenur felt that time had stood still. Nothing in the room had been touched. The dead woman's perfumes and jewelry were all spread on a dressing table as if she would be using them at any moment. Her nightgown and Davud's pajamas were folded casually at the foot of the bed. The woman's clothing was stacked in bundles in the closet next to some of Davud's clothing. On the floor her red embroidered slippers stood next to a pair of the colonel's soft leather house shoes.

Didenur felt a queasy feeling in the pit of her stomach. The state of this room explained Davud's indifference to her. He was obviously still deeply in love with his dead wife. And he was apparently clinging to the past and seeking emotional fulfillment in time spent in this room. So why did he re-marry before his emotional ties to his former wife had been laid to rest? Why did he marry Didenur?

That evening after dinner, Didenur questioned Davud about this.

"I saw your former wife's room today. You must still love her very much," said Didenur in a neutral tone of voice.

Davud looked surprised, but not upset. However, he did not respond to his wife's statement.

Didenur continued:

"It doesn't seem unusual to me that you love her, but why did you marry me?"

Davud averted Didenur's glance. He responded helplessly:

"I'm sorry, Didenur. I don't want to hurt you. But my mother insisted on my remarriage. She wants to see a grandson before she dies. I couldn't cross her. "

Didenur was shaken by the colonel's reply. So it had not been Davud's desire to remarry, but his mother's insistence that had led to their marriage. But what about Didenur's feelings and satisfaction in the relationship? Didn't they have any importance at all? Was Didenur only a vehicle for her mother-in-law's will? Did she have to sacrifice her feelings and well-being on the altar of her mother-in-law's desire for a grandson?

Didenur did not know what to think or say. She only felt intuitively that satisfying her mother-in-law's desire for a grandson was not a sufficient reason for conceiving a child. Moreover, what if she did conceive a child and it turned out to be a girl! How would her mother-in-law react to that? Didenur didn't even want to think about it. The woman had been completely oblivious to Didenur's emotional well-being in her obsession to get a grandson. How would she treat an innocent, vulnerable granddaughter whose only crime was not being a boy?

That night Didenur made no attempt to encourage Davud's closeness; she simply did not have it in her. She only felt numb.

After Didenur fell soundly asleep, she began to dream. She was surrounded by fog again like on the day she was captured when she was still a child in Circassia. The fog was so thick that she could almost hold it in her hands. She was searching for someone, but the fog held her back. It was a dark, damp wall that she was unable to penetrate. She knew that the person she was searching for was just beyond the fog, but for now she was unable to break through to him.

The next day the colonel returned to his military duty, and Didneur's life returned to its former routine. Again her days were filled with piano playing and teaching.

Several months later Didenur received an invitation from Aliye Sultan to visit the princess in Vanikoy. Didenur was delighted to accept the invitation. Not only would it be a welcome opportunity to break her daily routine, but she also wanted to see the princess very much. With ample time for contemplation due to the colonel being away from home so much, Didenur frequently thought about her years in the palace and her treasured friendship with Aliye Sultan and Servetseza. She missed both of them dearly. The joy and beauty of palace life seemed so far removed from her present life. Of course, she frequently visited with women from the neighborhood and she had as many students as she could handle, but her mother-in-law's negativity cast a dark shadow over Didenur's life. She looked forward to an outing when she could get away, if only for a day, from the gloom that loomed over her here.

Three days later on the day of the eagerly anticipated visit Didenur got up very early and put on one of her finest dresses. Although Didenur usually took care of her own hair, today she had her personal servant, Gulcemal, arrange her hair elegantly pinned up with costly hair combs. From among her jewelry, Didenur chose a ruby necklace and earrings which had been a part of her trousseau provided by the palace. After hurriedly sipping a small cup of Turkish coffee, Didenur put on her ferace and veil and, taking leave of her mother-in-law, she mounted the carriage that was waiting at the door. Gulcemal accompanied her and the two young women headed towards the closest dock from where the princess' royal caique and oarsmen would take them to Aliye Sultan's home in Vanikoy.

When Didenur descended from the carriage, she stopped for a moment to take in the exhilarating view of the Bosphorus. Docked nearby were several foreign freight ships and one Italian passenger ship. Small boats dotted the straits and the smell of fish hung in the air. Sea gulls soared overhead calling with shrill voices to one another. The crisp breeze seemed to blow away any remnants of remaining gloom, and Didenur suddenly felt fully alive again. She immediately spotted the flag identifying the royal caique and started to walk towards it. The princess' chief steward, Ismail Agah, a former agah at the imperial harem, remembered Didenur and helped her and Gulcemal board the boat. The curtains of the kiosk were tightly drawn, so Didenur could not enjoy the scenery as they crossed the straits, but just the smell of the sea was enough to make her feel refreshed and even a little giddy. The light caique quickly skimmed over the waters with the efforts of the skilled oarsmen, and the boat soon docked in front of the princess' mansion. As she entered the mansion, Didenur's thoughts turned to the princess' wedding. Everything had been so grand and elegant. She wondered if Aliye Sultan's life had changed as much as her own life had changed since then.

Didenur was shown into a smartly furnished sitting room overlooking the Bosphorus. Aliye Sultan's proclivity towards the West was evident in the flair with which the room was decorated. A Tonet seating group was located in front of the long windows looking out on the Straits and a Gaveau piano stood to the right. An Austrian clock and an elegant Meissen porcelain fruit bowl adorned an English-style console. Yet there was no scarcity of Ottoman-made elements in the room either. A large Hereke carpet covered most of the floor and the striped green and gold silk drapes were sewn from Hereke fabric. A white stove made from Turkish tiles and an Istanbul-crafted cabinet stood on the wall to the left. Didenur smiled to herself as she remembered that Aliye Sultan had always been at home in both worlds – the East and West.

Shortly, an elegantly dressed young slave girl entered the room and served coffee to Didenur. As she sipped the hot, foamy black coffee in an exquisitely decorated porcelain cup, Didenur saw the door open again. Expecting to see the princess enter, Didenur was amazed to find Servetseza standing in front of her. Hurriedly putting down her coffee cup, Didenur embraced Servetseza with excitement and elation. She was unable to restrain the tears of joy brimming over from her eyes. Didenur stood back and took a good look at her newly-found friend.

Much to her surprise, Didenur realized that Servetseza was pregnant. She was just about to ask her dear friend about her new life when the door opened again. This time it was Aliye Sultan. The two young women bowed before the princess who, in turn, gave them both a warm embrace that immediately put them at ease.

The three young women sat down at the dining table, which had been laid out in advance with elegant French Sevres porcelain china and Karlsbad crystal goblets. However, they were so absorbed in their conversation that no one noticed the elegant table setting or the exquisite Ottoman cuisine. Aliye Sultan questioned Servetseza about her new life:

"Tell me, my beautiful sister, have you been able to adjust easily to life outside the palace?

How do you spend your time? Are you happy with your marriage?"

Servetseza replied with a detailed description of her new life:

"My dear princess, I am very happy with my new life. My husband is a palace diplomat. He has a broad circle of acquaintances and a large extended family. My days are filled with entertaining the wives of other diplomats and visiting female relatives at innumerable family celebrations. Not a week passes without a ceremony in the family for a new baby or a circumcision or an engagement or wedding. And then there are frequent calls from the wives in our diplomatic circle and my return calls to them. Last week I hosted the wives of Austrian and Italian diplomats to the Ottoman Porte.

They were so curious about Ottoman women living in harems. I hope they weren't disappointed that my husband has only one wife!"

Aliye Sultan and Didenur both smiled at Servetseza's last remark. The Princess responded, "I know what you mean, my beautiful sister. Many Westerners come here intrigued by polygamy, and they are so disappointed when they learn how rare it is. They are also so eager to free us from harem life, although we women are quite content to be honored in the harem remote from the coarseness and difficulties of public life."

Looking at the princess' face, Didenur noticed that she had become quite pale. The concern obvious in her voice, Didenur asked:

"Oh, my sultan, are you feeling alright?"

"I'm fine, my dear sister; it's only a little morning sickness," the princess responded.

"Morning sickness!" exclaimed Servetseza. "Then you are expecting a baby, as well, my sultan?"

"Yes, my dear sisters, Alhamdulillah, I too am expecting a baby."

Didenur and Servetseza were overjoyed with the good news. They gave their sincere congratulations and best wishes for the new baby to come.

Turning towards Didenur, Aliye Sultan said, "Tell us, my sweet sister, what has your life been like since you left the palace?"

Didenur paused a moment. She didn't know what to say. It was unthinkable that she could lie to Aliye Sultan and Servetseza or try and cover up the truth. But she could not bring herself to articulate her problem with Davud and his mother either. She just remained silent for what seemed to be an eternity.

"Didenur…" said the princess in a compassionate and concerned tone of voice.

"Didenur!" Servetseza exclaimed with alarm.

Tears were welling up in Didenur's eyes and she suddenly began sobbing. It was as if all the pain and anguish that she had suppressed since her wedding night were pouring out from the depths of her being: the pain of not being loved and appreciated by her husband, the pain of being blamed unfairly by her mother-in-law for not becoming pregnant, and the anguish of dearly wanting a baby, but not wanting a baby from a loveless relationship. Didenur cried so hard that her whole body began to shake uncontrollably.

Aliye Sultan rubbed rose water on Didenur's face and hands to calm her down. Servetseza held her tightly until the deluge of tears began to subside. Slowly Didenur began to regain her composure. With difficulty, she explained her situation to the other two young women.

Servetseza was outraged by the situation:

"Didenur, you must get divorced immediately!"

Aliye Sultan took a more cautious approach:

"Didenur, search your heart carefully. If you decide to divorce, then I will insist upon your coming to my house to live. You are not alone and you can count on my support at all times."

Didenur was greatly comforted by the solid support of Aliye Sultan and Servetseza. The seeds of friendship that were planted in the palace when Didenur was a young girl had fallen on fertile ground and were now bearing precious fruit. Didenur truly was not alone. She knew she could rely on the princess and Servetseza under any circumstances.

The three young women continued talking for several hours. At times, they reminisced about the past; at times they shared their dreams for the future. When Didenur mentioned her piano students, Aliye Sultan insisted that she play for them on the Gaveau piano in the room. The past months of intense piano playing and teaching paid off well. The princess was genuinely impressed by the level of Didenur's accomplishment.

Unfortunately the time for leaving had arrived. The days were short and Servetseza and Didenur had to be home before sunset. Reluctantly bidding each other farewell and promising to meet again soon, Servetseza and Didenur took leave of Aliye Sultan and went their separate ways. Didenur and Gulcemal again boarded the princess's caique and returned to the other side of the Bosphorus. While skimming across the straits in the swift boat, Didenur thought about what the princess had said. She asked herself whether or not she should remain in this marriage, but she could not come up with a clear answer. She was very unhappy and there was no indication that things would get better anytime soon. On the other hand, she knew that life is full of trials. She decided to try and be patient until she had a clear sign as to which direction to take.

As the weeks and months progressed, the colonel's mother became more frustrated and demanding with each passing day. Her obsession to see a grandson before she died enveloped Didenur's life like a shirt of fire. Not one day passed without her rebuking Didenur for not bearing a grandson. She reproached Davud as well, but because he was in the field most of the time, Didenur received the brunt of her scorn.

One day after a particularly angry tirade of words, Didenur's mother-in-law told her that since Davud and Didenur had failed to produce a grandson, she was going to take things into her own hands. She left the house in a fury and returned an hour later with a middle-aged woman whose very appearance made Didenur shiver. Her arched eyebrows, pointed nose and several large boils on her face gave the woman a distinctly sinister air. She was clutching a black bundle close to her bosom as if someone might try and snatch it away. The two women hurried into the kitchen and chased out the cook who was preparing dinner. Didenur could hear them speaking in Serbian, but she could not understand what they said. Occasionally she heard the strange woman repeating what sounded like some kind of incantation.

A half an hour later the kitchen door opened and the stranger left without saying good-bye. Didenur's mother-in-law called her into the kitchen. As soon as Didenur entered the room she smelled a foul odor like rotten eggs. As Didenur looked around the room, she saw the source of the odor. It was a bowl containing a putrid concoction of unidentifiable ingredients sitting on the butcher's block. Didenur's mother-in-law pointed towards the bowl:

"Eat it," she said.

Didenur silently looked at the woman in amazement.

"Eat it," she repeated in a louder voice.

"I will not eat it," replied Didenur. "You cannot force me to do so."

Davud's mother became livid. She grabbed Didenur by the arm and violently pushed her towards the butcher's block. Didenur was caught off-guard. As she fell on the butcher's block, her arm hit the bowl, which fell to the floor with a crash. The foul concoction spilled everywhere.

Didenur's mother-in-law was beside herself. Shaking her trembling finger in Didenur's face, the exasperated woman shouted:

"You will not get away with this! You will pay for this disobedience! We will see who is in command when my son comes home tomorrow!"

Davud's mother rushed out the kitchen door with a vengeance. Not able to stand the stench which had permeated the whole kitchen, Didenur followed suit. She went straight to her room and stayed there to avoid any further encounter with her furious mother-in-law.

The next day the colonel returned home as expected. The door to their bedroom was open, so Didenur heard her husband's arrival. He no more than got through the door than his mother began bombarding him with her complaints. Didenur heard her name repeated several times in the vengeful woman's harangue, but she could not follow her words specifically because Davud's mother was speaking in her native tongue. At any rate, the topic of the discussion needed no explanation; Didenur knew her mother-in-law's complaints by heart.

This time, however, there was a new twist to the woman's tirade of words. Waving three fingers in the air, the colonel's mother was commanding him to take action. Davud looked shocked and his face turned pale, but he nodded his head "yes."

Davud slowly walked towards the bedroom he shared with Didenur. Finding his wife sitting on the sofa, the colonel cleared his throat before speaking. Turning towards Didenur, but not looking her in the eyes, Davud said in a shaky voice:

"Didenur… Didenur, I divorce you. I divorce you. I divorce you…"

Didenur was too stunned to speak.

The colonel continued:

"Of course, I'll make sure you are set up comfortably elsewhere. I'll pay your deferred mahr."

Again avoiding eye contact, he said:

"Didenur, I'm sorry, but I cannot act against my mother's wishes."

A bitter smile crossed Didenur's face as she thought ironically how appropriate an ending this was to her marriage. Her mother-in-law had ordained this marriage to be and she had ordained it to end. Didenur and Davud had merely been the lead players in this drama, the meaning and wisdom of which Didenur could not yet begin to fathom.

CHAPTER 7

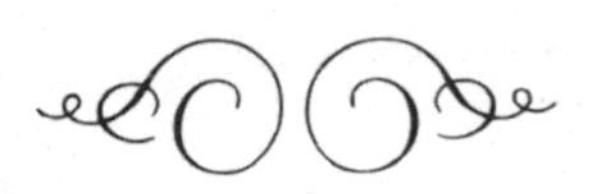

Beylerbeyi 1867

Preparing to go out shopping for some jewelry for Ziya's fiance, Jamila looked at her hair carefully in the mirror. She decided to apply some henna as soon as possible, because the grey strands in her hair were becoming more and more obvious. The events of the past year -the death of her beloved parents in a cholera epidemic- had taken a heavy toll on Jamila's health and appearance. Although she was still strikingly beautiful, the radiance that had once shown in her face had begun to fade. As always, it was Jamila who had nursed her parents during their illness. Putting her own life on the line, she had cared for them day and night with the assistance of Gulshah Dadı and the other servants. But in spite of Jamila's utmost care and prayers, she was unable to save them from the ravages of cholera. Her mother, Safiye Hanım, had passed on to life in the next world a little more than a year ago and her father, Hikmet Efendi, had followed her six days later. It seemed like yesterday. The pain and sorrow she had felt at their deaths was as fresh and deep as ever. It was only that now, with Ziya's approaching marriage, she had many other things to preoccupy her mind.

It was Jamila who had to make most of the wedding arrangements. Kamil was away from home a great deal of the time, and when he was at home he was very aloof. He was basically disengaged from the events that were taking place around him, even the upcoming marriage of his only son. Kamil had never achieved the professional success that he had hoped for. After the death of his parents many years ago, his career seemed to be put on hold, and he was unable to advance beyond the position of first assistant to the head physician at the palace. There had been two different head physicians appointed in the last ten years, but Kamil was always overlooked when a vacancy arose. This situation devastated Kamil. His preoccupation with his professional obsession and his failure to become chief physician at the imperial palace negatively impacted his personal relations, especially his relationship with Jamila.

In the absence of a fulfilling dialogue with Kamil in the past several years, Jamila had turned to Ziya for support and companionship. Her son had responded whole-heartedly. Their relationship had always been a very close one. Even as a child Ziya had been wise beyond his years. Jamila had been amazed on numerous occasions at how easily Ziya comprehended everything she said. She never had to explain twice. Later on, while training to become an architect, Ziya had also amazed his teachers with his profound comprehension of architectural design and the metaphysics underlying it.

Jamila was able to confer with Ziya on any and every subject, a situation which gave her great comfort. He had been particularly strong and supportive to his mother during the illness of his grandparents, more so than even his father. As a doctor, Kamil Bey had given medical instruction, but he was too absorbed in his own inner world to be able to give Jamila the emotional and psychological support she needed to pull through this trauma of loss. It was Ziya who always saved his mother from falling into the depths of despair and who helped her maintain her emotional and psychological balance.

Now Jamila wanted to do her best for Ziya. She wanted his wedding to be as perfect as possible. A month ago Ziya had become engaged to a lovely young girl named Nilufer who lived in a large Ottoman house across the street from Kamil Bey and

Jamila's mansion. The families had known each other for many years and there had been a tacit understanding between them for a long time that Ziya and Nilufer would eventually marry. As young children they had played together during family visits, and the two had attended the same primary school attached to the Beylerbeyi mosque. But once Nilufer reached puberty and began to wear a ferace and veil, social interaction between them was no longer permissible. Only occasional glimpses of one another while leaving and entering their houses were possible now. This situation, however, did not dampen their feelings for one another; in fact, it enhanced them.

Unable to communicate verbally with Nilufer, Ziya expressed his love for Nilufer through poetry. He was careful, however, not to overstep the bounds of propriety in his poetry. He never addressed Nilufer directly, but always expressed his feelings through metaphor. Ziya disregarded the rules of propriety, however, when he had Nilufer's younger brother Naim secretly smuggle the poems to his sister. Nilufer read and reread the poems at night by candlelight after everyone else had gone to bed.

Their engagement had been postponed almost a year with the death of Jamila's parents. But now Jamila wanted to proceed with the wedding plans without further delay. Engagement gifts had been exchanged between the families; Nilufer's ring and the material for her bridal dress had been sent immediately after the engagement. The newlyweds were to live with Kamil and Jamila, and the private suite in their home, where she and Kamil had stayed when they first married, was redecorated. Almost all arrangements had been completed for the wedding celebration, which was to take place ten days later, a week after the official marriage ceremony. Jamila had had an elegant, midnight blue silk caftan made for the occasion. Although she had no desire or interest in new clothing, she wanted to look her best for Ziya. Today she planned to complete her final major task –buying a necklace, which she would present to Nilufer at the official marriage ceremony three days later. It had to be something very special. Jamila wanted Nilufer to know how much she valued her son's bride-to-be.

Jamila put on her ferace and covered her face with two transparent white veils, as was the custom of the time. The first veil covered her hair and forehead and the second one covered her face from below the eyes to below the chin. She tied both of them at the back of her neck. Two of her servants accompanied her and they went down a set of stairs under the house, which descended to a small, private dock. There the chief foreman and eight oarsman were waiting in a large caique to carry their mistress and the women servants across the Bosphorus Straits to Eminonu, where the foreman would hire a carriage to take the women to the Covered Bazaar.

As the boat set out to cross the straits, Jamila's eyes scanned the houses along the shores. She couldn't imagine anything more beautiful. Magnificent wooden *yalıs* or shore houses painted in pastel colors dotted the green coastline. Nestled in broad gardens filled with fruit trees, fountains and flowers, the houses had a most enticing appearance. Unlike many houses facing each other on the streets, with their windows covered by wooden latticed shutters for privacy, these houses facing the water had only white lace curtains at the open windows which were occasionally ruffled by the summer breeze. A stately old plane tree standing in her neighbor's garden caught Jamila's attention. It appeared to be hundreds of years old. She wondered what stories it would tell if only it could speak.

The water had a calming effect on Jamila. A host of sweet memories surfaced: boat excursions with her parents, fishing on the dock with her father when she was a child, swimming with her girl friends underneath one of the shore houses as a teenager. Her life with her parents had been full and rich, like a beautiful tapestry interwoven with love and joy. The first half of her married years had been happy and fulfilling, too. It was only after the death of Kamil's parents that her relationship with Kamil had begun to skid. She wondered if they had hit rock bottom, or was the worse still to come.

Jamila felt helpless in regard to her marital relationship. As she understood it, the main problem lay with Kamil's perception of reality rather than with reality itself. In Kamil's mind he was a failure because he had not attained the position of chief physician in the palace. In reality, however, most people saw Kamil as a successful assistant chief physician, a position admired and envied by many. He had a devoted wife and a jewel of a son, more wealth than he needed, and a sound position among the Ottoman elite. He had good health, good looks and a winning personality – blessings not to be taken for granted by anyone. Yet, the fact that he had not obtained his goal made him feel insecure and powerless. Had he counted his blessings and looked at the full half of the glass instead of the empty half, he could have been a grateful and satisfied man. Jamila had tried to explain this to Kamil many times and to convince him of the truth of it, but to no avail. Kamil just receded further and further into his shell, seeing himself as the victim of a capricious fate.

At first Jamila had resisted her situation and she had struggled hard to regain the happy relationship she and Kamil once had. But after failing time and again to make any progress whatsoever, she finally decided to accept the situation and focus on other things in her life. She had become even more devoted to her son Ziya and, fortunately, she had spent a lot of time with her parents in their last years. After their deaths, knowing that she had given her utmost to them in the final years of their lives helped to assuage her pain. Now she treasured the memories of the time they had spent together. For a long time after their deaths it had been hard for Jamila to accept that she would never see them again in this world. It seemed that they had just gone away temporarily, like when they went to visit distant relatives. But slowly in time the reality of death began to sink in: her parents no longer existed on this plane.

The small boat skimmed over the straits with ease. As Jamila looked out over the sparkling water glistening under the rays of the sun, she saw two dolphins swimming and leaping into the air a little ways off. She was startled at first, but then she saw the look on their faces. It almost seemed as though the dolphins were smiling at her. Momentarily forgetting about her troubles, Jamila smiled back. She felt the dolphins were a good omen.

The caique continued cutting through the water and soon approached the Eminonu dock. After a few careful maneuvers, it was secured tightly to a wooden post. The foreman leaped out first and then assisted the women to step out of the boat. He hired one of the colorfully decorated carriages standing nearby and helped the women get in. Then he sat up front next to the driver. The horse-drawn carriage wound slowing through the crowded streets until it stopped in front of the Covered Bazaar. Leaving the foreman at the entrance, the women entered the bazaar. The colorful, lively atmosphere inside never failed to enchant Jamila.

There were endless rows of shops with every imaginable kind of merchandise – heaps of pungent spices from distant lands; colorful hand-woven carpets with the most intricate designs; carefully crafted wooden shelves and stools with inlaid mother-of-pearl; large porcelain containers of sweets, halva and candy; beautifully embroidered scarves and covers; handsomely embossed leather items like cushions and saddle-bags; delicately engraved copper, silver and brass household ware, etc. It was a feast of unique and varied sights, sounds and smells.

Passing by a long row of shops selling silk goods, Jamila and her attendants turned the corner onto a row of goldsmith shops. Shimmering in large glass display cases, the gold jewelry and precious stones emanated light in an otherwise dim environment. Jamila continued walking down the long corridor of goldsmith shops until she came to her cousin Mehmet's location. Jamila not only fully trusted her cousin, but she also highly valued Mehmet's fine aesthetic taste. She always bought her jewelry from him, and she had never been disappointed.

As soon as Mehmet Bey saw Jamila and her attendants, he sent the errand boy to bring them some tea. Speaking in a warm tone of voice, but avoiding eye-contact, Mehmet Bey first inquired about Kamil and Ziya.

"Jamila Hanım, I trust that the honorable and distinguished Kamil Efendi and your noble son Ziya are in good health."

"God willing, they are sound and well," replied Jamila. "And how about my venerable uncle and your lovely wife Aisha," Jamila asked in return.

Assured that they were fine, she opened the topic of wedding preparations. Jamila described the type of jewelry she had in mind. Mehmet Bey opened a locked metal chest and took out two small bundles from inside. He carefully unwrapped the cloth cover concealing the jewelry in the first bundle. It contained an exquisite necklace made from five interwoven rows of small emeralds and diamonds. While Jamila was examining the necklace at closer range, her cousin unwrapped the second bundle, which contained a magnificent gold filigree necklace set with seven large fire rubies. Jamila put the first necklace down and picked up the ruby necklace. Both were works of perfection. Each was unique in its own way, and Jamila could not decide between them.

"And what are these beauties worth, my dear cousin," asked Jamila, hoping that she might decide between them on the basis of their cost.

"Money is not important. As long as you like them, Kamil Efendi and I will settle on a reasonable price," replied Mehmet Bey.

Jamila could not choose between them. Then she remembered the two smiling dolphins and decided to buy both pieces of jewelry. She would give one necklace right away as a wedding present. The other she would set aside until the birth of her first grandchild and then give it to her daughter-in-law as a gift of appreciation.

Jamila expressed her heartfelt thanks to her cousin and left his shop with a feeling of elation. The preparations for Ziya's marriage were now complete.

Jamila returned home from the Covered Bazaar the same way she had come. As the caique sailed swiftly over the waters, Jamila kept an eye out for the dolphins, but they were no where in sight. Soon the boat drew up to their private dock and Jamila and her attendants got out and went up the stairs to the house. Ziya was curiously waiting for his mother's return.

"Do you bring good news, Anneciğim?" asked Ziya with a grin on his face.

"Beautiful news," replied Jamila. "In fact, it's twice as good as you were expecting," she added, smiling to herself.

Jamila took the necklaces out of their soft, velvet covers. The jewels sparkled as the light hit them.

"But I thought it was custom to give one necklace. Anne, are we starting a new tradition?" Ziya asked teasingly as he admired both pieces of jewelry.

"No, my dear son, we are not starting a new tradition. Your mother was unable to decide between the two necklaces, so she bought them both. One for now and one for the birth of her first grandchild."

"Grandchild! Anneciğim, please slow down. I'm not even married yet!" exclaimed Ziya.

"But you will be soon, Ziya. And, God willing, a child will follow in due time. You have been the greatest blessing of my life, and I want you, too, to experience the bond of love a parent feels for a child."

Giving his mother a warm smile, Ziya said softly, "Thank you, Anne, for always thinking of my well-being."

Three days later on the day of the official marriage ceremony Jamila woke up before dawn. After performing the morning ritual prayer, she sat for a long time on the prayer rug, imploring God to make Ziya's marriage a blessed one. She felt sad that her parents could not be there to witness this happy event… Yet she knew that life had to go on without them. So she held back the tears welling up in her eyes and turned her thoughts to Ziya and Nilufer.

Jamila felt that she was gaining a daughter with Nilufer. She had known the bride-to-be since she was a small child and she truly loved her. Nilufer was innately elegant and refined. She was as lovely as her Persian namesake –the water lily. Jamila had diligently cultivated her relationship with the young girl over the years, taking care not to hurt her in any way. In her heart Jamila had already accepted Nilufer as her daughter; the official marriage ceremony would simply formalize the relationship.

Shortly Jamila heard Ziya's footsteps. She immediately went to see how her son was doing on this important day. Jamila followed Ziya to the main sitting room and found him standing in front of a large bay window looking out over the Bosphorus Straits. Hearing his mother enter the room, Ziya turned around. His face was profoundly serene.

"Anne, shouldn't you rest a little more? Today will be a very busy day for all of us."

"And I don't want to miss a minute of it! My only son does not get married every day," replied Jamila animatedly. "You know, Ziya, today is the beginning of a new phase in your life –new responsibilities, new challenges, new joys. There will of course be trials along with the pleasures, but I want you to know with certainty that I will be at your side every step of the way."

"I have no doubt about that, Anneciğim," Ziya responded with love and appreciation in his eyes. "You always have been. You've been the main pillar of strength in our family. You always pick me up when I fall down. I was just thinking about what a fortunate man I am to have two wonderful women in my life like you and Nilufer. I am truly blessed."

"You love Nilufer deeply, don't you Ziya?" Jamila asked.

"With all my heart, Anne. She's the only woman I've ever even thought of as a wife."

"May Allah bless both of you with a long and fruitful marriage, my son," Jamila said. And recalling her own troublesome marriage, she added, "May the joy you feel now continue until death parts your ways."

Their intimate talk was interrupted by a knock on the door. It was a servant bringing their morning coffee. Sitting down to drink their coffee at a *téte-a-téte* table, Jamila and Ziya became engrossed in the mesmerizing early morning beauty of the straits.

Shortly another servant announced that breakfast was ready. Following traditional Turkish custom, a large brass tray was brought in and set up in the room. Seating herself on a floor cushion, Jamila asked the kalfa where Kamil Efendi was. The servant replied that he had left to make a medical call the previous evening and that he had not yet returned. This news upset Jamila very much. Kamil had been spending more and more time away from home in recent months. But today was the day of his son's official marriage. Soon they would have to go to the bride's home for the ceremony. Was he going to be late for his son's marriage??? Concealing her anger as best she could, Jamila began eating breakfast with Ziya; but she had difficulty swallowing the food…

After breakfast, Jamila went to her room to get dressed. Gulshah Dadı was busy preparing Jamila's wedding apparel, but she looked up when the door opened. Jamila smiled at the aging woman. Gulshah Dadı had slowed down perceptibly, but Jamila would not consider having her replaced. It had been the dadı's request to remain in Jamila's service, although she could have left whenever she wanted. Her nine-year term of service had expired long ago, but she could not imagine herself anyplace except at Jamila's side. She had no desire to live anywhere except with Jamila and her family who had truly become her own family. She planned to remain with them until she died.

Jamila, too, was very happy with this arrangement. Gulshah Dadı was her strongest living link with her childhood and parents. They often reminisced about events from Jamila's past. Gulshah Dadı knew Jamila better than anyone else. Although Jamila had a smile on her face, Gulshah Dadı could sense the tension underneath. She knew Jamila was totally in favor of Ziya's marriage, so the problem was probably Kamil Efendi. He had become a source of increasing anxiety for Jamila.

Trying to divert Jamila's attention, Gulshah Dadı said, "It seems like yesterday that Ziya Bey was born. Do you remember what a sweet little boy he was? So easy to care for."

"Ziya has truly lived up to his name," replied Jamila. "He has been the light of my life, Gulshah Dadı, everything a mother could wish from her child. I want today to be perfect for him. He deserves the very best."

"I think he's getting the best. Nilufer Hanım is a real prize. You can be sure she will do her best to make Ziya Bey happy," Gulshah Dadı added. She noticed that Jamila's face had relaxed a little. But how long would it last?

After Jamila finished dressing, she took the velvet bag with the emerald necklace in it and proceeded downstairs where Ziya was waiting for her. Just as they were leaving the house, Kamil Efendi's carriage pulled up to the front gate. As they passed each other at the gate, Kamil Efendi said that he would come as soon as he changed clothes. Jamila said nothing, but she gave him an entreating look as if to say, "Please don't let Ziya down today!"

Nilufer and her family were expectantly waiting for the groom and his parents. Also the imam and two close neighbors who would act as witnesses had already arrived. Everyone was there except Kamil Efendi. The men sat in the main hall of the selamlık section of the house and the women sat in an adjacent room. While they were waiting for Kamil to arrive, Jamila took the opportunity to present the necklace to Nilufer.

"It's exquisite," said Nilufer as Jamila took the necklace out of its velvet cover. "I've never seen anything so beautiful."

"It's just a token of our love for you, Nilufer. May you wear it with joy?"

Nilufer's mother and the wives of the two witnesses admired the necklace in glowing words as Jamila put it around Nilufer's neck. Jamila stepped back and took a good look at the necklace. It both enhanced and was enhanced by Nilufer's beauty. Seeing the flush of excitement on the young bride's face, Jamila recalled the happiness she had felt on her own wedding day. The remembrance of that day's joy only made her present sadness all the more acute. What dark shadow had fallen between her and her husband?

The sound of Kamil's voice brought Jamila back to the moment. After an exchange of greetings among the men, the official marriage ceremony began. It was a simple ceremony. The marriage contract had already been prepared well in advance. Generous sums had been fixed for Nilufer's mahr and daily allowance. The imam read the contract and asked both Nilufer and Ziya if it was acceptable. Receiving positive answers, the imam signed the contract as did both parties and the witnesses. Now it only remained to be registered at court. Ziya's family would make the initial payment of the mahr within a few days time, and the events leading up to the consummation of the marriage would begin the following Monday with the transfer of Nilufer's trousseau across the street to her new home.

Everyone congratulated each other and wished future happiness for the bride and groom. As she kissed her daughter-in-law on the forehead, Jamila saw tears of joy in Nilufer's eyes. They mirrored the tears of joy in Jamila's own eyes. Dinner trays were brought into both rooms and the carefully prepared banquet began. Nilufer's mother, Zainab Hanım, had spared no effort in the preparation of the meal. At least twenty different dishes –from appetizers and soup to main courses and desserts- had been made by the cooks with seasoned culinary skill. The lengthy meal was topped off with an audible feast of instrumental Turkish classical music.

The sun had already set when Jamila asked for permission to leave. After a repetition of congratulations and well wishes, she waited at the door for Kamil and Ziya to escort her across the street. Ziya appeared and beckoned his mother to cross the street with him:

"Anneciğim, let me give you a hand. We'll cross the street together," Ziya offered.

"Where's your father, Ziya? Shouldn't we wait for him?" Jamila asked.

"He left," replied Ziya. "He excused himself half-way through the musical concert due to an urgent need at the palace for his medical services."

Jamila was stunned by this news. She had hoped in vain that Kamil would give his full attention to Ziya today and put his son before his work. Although she pretended there was nothing unusual about this situation, Jamila's heart was deeply wounded…

The initial payment of mahr was promptly sent to the bride, and the marriage festivities began the next Monday. Nilufer's trousseau was carried to her new home in large bundles tied with red ribbons perched on the heads of immaculately dressed male servants. Larger items like trunks and pieces of furniture were rolled across the street on wooden carts. Although the path of the bridal procession was quite short, this did not prevent vendors and children from standing in their way until they were paid some coins. A large group of Nilufer's female relatives and friends arrived to set up the bridal display. The women and girls worked diligently until the bridal suite was fully prepared for the wedding celebration.

Seeing the bridal throne being decorated with elegant scarves and shawls, Jamila couldn't help but look back to the time when her bridal throne had been made. Those were truly glorious days to remember, but now the roles had changed and she would be welcoming the new bride into her home. And Jamila thought that was just as it should be. Everything in life is in a continuous state of change and re-creation: young girls become brides, brides become mothers, and mothers become grandmothers. Now it was time for Jamila to enjoy the warmth and golden beauty of autumn, while Nilufer basked in the glory and effervescence of spring.

On Tuesday, the new bride was taken to the public bath where a bridal celebration took place among female relatives, neighbors and friends. Nilufer was scrubbed and shampooed in preparation for her wedding night. The festivities lasted all day. There was singing, dancing, music and dining until late afternoon when the women all left to be home before dark.

According to the traditional timetable of Ottoman weddings, on Wednesday Jamila and her female relatives would be hosted by the women of Nilufer's family and that night would be the night of henna when Nilufer said good-bye to her childhood friends. But unlike many brides, Nilufer did not feel the slightest bit of sadness. Because the families of the bride and groom had been friends and neighbors for many years, Nilufer's marriage would not bring drastic change to her life. She was just moving across the street, well within distance of her own family. Also she had known her new family for most of her life. Nilufer had long since learned to love and respect her in-laws, especially Jamila Hanım who had always been like a second mother to her. And as for Ziya… he was the sun of her life. How could she feel anything but joy about marrying Ziya?

On Thursday Nilufer would be taken to her new home by Ziya's family. Early in the morning all the women of the neighborhood began to collect in front of Nilufer's house in anticipation of seeing the young bride in her wedding dress. They were not disappointed. Before long, relatives from far and near began to arrive to escort the bride to her new home. Together with Jamila and Kamil Efendi, all were shown into large sitting rooms and served coffee and sweets.

Nilufer appeared shortly in an elegant white lace-wedding gown with a satin cape. Breaking with tradition, she had used a Parisian model for her wedding dress.

Once the guests had finished their coffee, they escorted the bride across the street where Ziya was waiting to meet her. Ziya took Nilufer's arm and accompanied her to the bridal throne. He raised Nilufer's veil and looked into his bride's eyes with deep love and passion. Trembling with excitement, Nilufer returned his gaze.

"My love, at last we are together. Thank God, the years of waiting are over," Ziya said.

But before Nilufer could respond, female guests began to pour into the bridal chamber to congratulate the new bride. Ziya excused himself and went to attend to the male guests in the selamlık. Nilufer thanked her guests one by one and kissed the hands of the elderly women, many of whom were women from the neighborhood who had known Nilufer all her life.

That evening when the newlyweds were finally alone, their years of yearning heightened their moment of union and elevated their bliss to a plane neither of them had ever experienced before.

Holding Nilufer in his arms, Ziya said tenderly, "*Birtanem,* * you've filled my emptiness and made me whole. You've given my life new meaning."

"Ziya, you *are* my life," Nilufer responded.

The couple spent the night enraptured in their new-found intimacy. The sun had already started to rise when they drifted off to sleep in each others arms.

Celebrations continued for two full days. The doors of the mansion were open to rich and poor alike and no one was turned away from the wedding banquet. Musicians and dancers entertained the guests to ensure that everyone enjoyed themselves. It was a communal event where the joy of the bride and groom were shared

---

* A term of endearment meaning, "My one and only."

by everyone and where prayers and well-wishes abounded for the happiness of the newlyweds.

The day after the wedding celebrations ended, Ziya and Nilufer set sail on a two-week steamship cruise in the Mediterranean Sea. Jamila had thought it would be a perfect time for her and Kamil to take a sea cruise as well; they desperately needed to re-open their channels of communication and allow some fresh life to flow into their relationship. As they were seeing the newlyweds off, Jamila made the suggestion:

"Kamil Efendi, we're both exhausted from the wedding preparations and celebrations. I was wondering if the two of us might get away for a week or two while Ziya and Nilufer are gone… a sea cruise perhaps?"

Without hesitating Kamil replied:

"I'm sorry, Jamila. I really would like to, but I don't think I can get away from my work at this time. Maybe another time."

CHAPTER 8

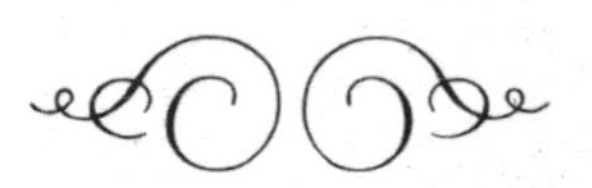

Beylerbeyi 1867

Jamila basically spent the next two weeks in the quietude of her home, although in the afternoons there were frequent visits from friends and neighbors who came to give their congratulations. It was a time of contemplation for Jamila, a time when she did a lot of soul-searching. Until recently, Jamila's roles in life had been clear cut. Her agenda had been basically oriented towards her family. She had been a caring daughter to her parents as long as they were alive. And she was a dedicated wife to her husband and a compassionate mother to her son. But now her parents no longer needed her care. Ziya had a partner who could fulfill many of the tasks Jamila had been doing. And as for Kamil, he had closed the door to his inner world. It was not possible for Jamila to be deeply involved in his life; she was only on the perimeter. This situation unnerved her. For the first time in her life Jamila felt unsure of her place in this world, as if the ground under her feet was shifting.

Jamila was relieved when Ziya and Nilufer returned home. Their presence allowed her to push the uneasiness she felt to the back of her mind. Nilufer's constant companionship prevented Jamila from asking herself too many questions. Her life became more action oriented: many places to go and people to visit. Plus there was a constant stream of guests who wanted to see the new bride. The heady activity continued for several months until one evening at dinner when Ziya gave his mother some startling news:

"Anneciğim, what did you do with my baby crib when I grew out of it?"

"I think we put it in the attic, Ziya. Why do you ask?" responded Jamila.

With a broad smile on his face, Ziya answered, "God willing, we're going to need it. Nilufer is expecting our first child."

Jamila was caught off guard. She could hardly believe her ears. Somehow she had not expected a baby so soon, perhaps because she had been married two years before Ziya was conceived. But she was thrilled with the news. The baby would give her life a new purpose and a new role: doting grandmother.

Jamila and Nilufer immediately began preparing for the new baby. The crib was brought down from the attic and sent to a carpentry shop to be refurbished. New linens, towels and baby clothes were sewn by all the women in the harem. The Beylerbeyi mansion took on new life.

As the months passed, Nilufer had to spend more and more time resting due to her delicate constitution. No one minded, however, because they were all eager to assist the mother-to-be.

Jamila watched over her with an eagle eye. She wanted to make sure that Nilufer's pregnancy passed in the best and safest possible way. She even requested that Kemal Efendi spend more time at home during the final months, even though arrangements had been made for an experienced midwife to deliver the baby.

One night three weeks before the baby was due Jamila woke up in the middle of the night to the sound of knocking at her door. When she got up and opened the door, she found Ziya standing there. His face was distraught.

"Anne, come quickly," Ziya said. "Nilufer is having severe pains."

Jamila grabbed her robe and hurriedly put it on as she quickly passed down the corridor to Ziya and Nilufer's suite. She ran to Nilufer's side and learned that her water had broken. Jamila told Ziya to immediately summon the foreman and have him dispatch one servant to bring the midwife and another to send news to Kamil Efendi who was on duty at the palace that night. He should also inform Nilufer's mother, Zainab Hanım. Ziya quickly went downstairs to call the foreman. Jamila sat down next to Nilufer and tried to comfort her.

"It looks like our baby is in a hurry to enter this world," said Jamila softly stroking the young woman's hair.

Nilufer was about to answer when her body was seized by a contraction.

"Breathe deeply," Jamila continued. "It will help the contraction to subside."

Ziya returned to the room. "Don't worry, *hayatım*,* help is on the way. I've sent for the midwife. She should be here soon. Also I've sent word to my father to come as quickly as possible."

Nilufer's smile was broken by another contraction. She held on tightly to Jamila's and Ziya's hands. Beads of sweat broke out on the young woman's forehead.

Jamila tried to comfort her daughter-in-law:

"I know your pain is great, Nilufer, but you will forget all about the labor pains once you hold your baby in your arms. Try and focus on that miraculous moment."

There was the sound of voices outside the bedroom door and Jamila immediately got up and opened it. It was Zainab Hanım and the midwife, Mansure Bajı, along with Gulshah Dadı and several other female servants. Jamila welcomed Zainab Hanım and told her there was nothing to worry about. Mansure Bajı politely asked Ziya to wait in the sitting room. After examining Nilufer, she confirmed that the birth process had begun, but she also added that there was still plenty of time before the baby would be born. Jamila was relieved to hear that because it would give Kamil Efendi ample time to arrive.

---

* A term of endearment meaning "My life."

The servants brought all the cloths and necessary items that had been prepared in advance, as well as swaddling clothes and blankets for the newborn. Everything appeared to be under control. The women tried to make Nilufer as comfortable as possible. Her mother wiped the sweat from her forehead with a damp cloth, and one of the servants sprinkled rose water on her head and hands.

Jamila stayed at Nilufer's side for four–five hours. She kept expecting Kamil to arrive at any moment. When he did not, she decided to go and ask Ziya about the matter. Leaving Nilufer with her mother and the midwife, Jamila went to find Ziya. He was in the sitting room reading the Quran.

"Anneciğim, how is Nilufer? Is the birth going well?" he asked.

"Everything is normal so far. Mansure Bajı said the baby should be born within a few hours," replied Jamila. "Ziya have you heard anything from your father? I was expecting him before now."

"I sent Rajab Agah to bring him here, but he came back two hours ago and said they were not able to locate Baba at the palace."

"That's strange," said Jamila. "How can they overlook your father?"

Although it hurt Jamila to see Nilufer in pain, she returned to her side immediately to offer any support she could. Nilufer looked exhausted. However, at least the interval between the contractions had shortened. Jamila again held Nilufer's hand, and at the same time she was silently praying for everything to turn out well.

Three hours later the baby's head appeared and the birth went quickly after that. It was a perfect baby girl. Although she was a little smaller than she would have been if she had waited the full term, still the baby was in perfect health. The midwife cut the umbilical cord and turned the baby over to Jamila and Gulshah Dadı to wash.

Jamila was elated! What a miracle she had just witnessed! She and the dadı carefully cleaned the newborn with warm water and wrapped her up securely to give the baby to her mother. As

Jamila turned around to give the baby to Nilufer, the midwife told her to wait.

Mansure Bajı and Zainab Hanım both had serious looks of concern on their faces. Jamila was confused about what was happening until she looked down and saw that the sheet underneath Nilufer was soaked with blood. Mansure Bajı immediately took an herbal remedy from her bag and put it on Nilufer's tongue. Then she waited five-ten minutes for the remedy to take affect. But the bleeding continued. The midwife gave Nilufer another dose of the remedy and waited ten minutes more. But the bleeding still continued. Then Mansure Bajı took a different remedy from her bag and put it in Nilufer's mouth. But after waiting another ten minutes, she saw that it had no affect either. Extra sheets were brought to absorb the profuse blood. Nilufer was hemorrhaging badly. Her face had become pale and translucent. Zainab Hanım was imploring God to save her daughter.

An acute feeling of fear seized Jamila's heart, a feeling she had felt when she first realized that she was losing her parents. She looked down at the baby girl in her arms. She prayed with all her being that this baby not lose its mother. But despite all the efforts of Mansure Bajı, the hemorrhaging continued. Nilufer weakened more and more each moment. Zainab Hanım was crying. Jamila gave the baby to Gulshah Dadı and ran to call Ziya.

"Ziya, Ziya, you must come at once," she exclaimed as she ran into the sitting room.

"Anne, what is it? Is there something wrong with the baby?" Ziya asked anxiously.

Jamila did not answer him. She just ran back to the room with Ziya close behind. When they got to the door they heard the sound of women weeping. By the time they entered the room, Nilufer had closed her eyes for the last time. At first, Ziya could not comprehend what he saw. Jamila took the baby from Gulshah Dadı and put her in Ziya's arms. Seeing that the baby was alive and well, he understood that everyone was crying for Nilufer. Ziya hurried to Nilufer's side. Her body was as warm as usual. However, when the midwife checked her pulse, there was no longer a heartbeat.

Jamila motioned for the midwife and servants to leave for now to allow Ziya a few moments alone with Nilufer. Grief-stricken, Zainab Hanım and Jamila followed them out the door. Jamila offered to take the baby from Ziya's arms, but Ziya clung tightly to his daughter – she was all the life that Ziya had left from Nilufer.

Jamila immediately called the foreman and told him to inform Nilufer's family of the death and she also told him to inform the neighbors that they had an urgent need for a wet nurse. At the same time she instructed Gulshah Dadı to later on bring material which was stored in a chest in the attic for a winding sheet. Nilufer's body would have to be washed and prepared for burial.

Hearing the baby's cry, Jamila went to Ziya's side. Tears were streaming down Ziya's face as well, falling onto the baby's blanket. Jamila took the crying baby and turned it over to Gulshah Dadı. Then she went back to Ziya's side and embraced him. She hugged her son with all her might. Jamila felt sobs of grief rising in her own chest, but she forced them back. She had to be strong for Ziya. If she lost control of her emotions, she knew it was likely that Ziya would follow suit. In her heart she called on God for strength. This was a moment of sore trial for Jamila: she felt profound grief for Nilufer's death; she felt vast compassion for Ziya's pain; and she felt deep sorrow for the motherless baby. She also felt some anger towards Kamil…

Jamila held Ziya in her arms. Tears were streaming down their faces, but they did not speak. "The point where words end…" Jamila had heard that expression before, but she had not fully understood it. Now she and Ziya were at that point. No words could express the depth of their loss…

There was a knock at the door. It was Gulshah Dadı. A wet nurse had been found for the baby and Jamila was needed to give her approval. Also the rest of Nilufer's family had arrived and neighbors had begun to come to give their condolences. Jamila gently told Ziya to wash his face. Duty awaited him in the selamlık. He would need to accept the condolences of male visitors.

After Ziya left the room, Jamila instructed the mid-wife and several servants to wash Nilufer's body, as was custom, before wrapping her in a shroud. She also designated one of the servants to read the Quran at Nilufer's side. Then she went to attend to the baby and the wet nurse. Jamila approved of the young woman and went with her to the nursery to oversee the baby's first feeding.

While Jamila was in the nursery, Kamil Efendi came home. As his carriage approached the gate of the mansion, he was puzzled by the stream of people entering and leaving his house.

"*Hayrola,*"* said Kamil Efendi as he walked through the gate.

"*Başınız sağ olsun,*"** said Nedim Efendi, one of Kamil's neighbors. "We are so sorry about the death of your daughter-in-law. If there is anything we can do, please let us know."

Kamil was frozen in his tracks. How could Nilufer be dead, he had just seen her the day before at breakfast. There must be some kind of horrible mistake. Kamil Efendi saw Rajab Agah coming out the door of the selamlık. He called him over.

"*Başınız sağ olsun, Kamil Efendi,*" said the foreman in a quiet voice.

"Rajab Agah, what's going on here? Please tell me what has happened," replied Kamil.

The elderly servant explained as much as he knew about Nilufer's death. He also mentioned that the new baby was a girl. Kamil was crushed by the news of Nilufer's death. He felt he should have

---

* "Hopefully everything is well."

** "May you be spared." (A form of condolence.)

been here last night; perhaps he could have prevented her death. He blamed this tragedy on himself.

Rather than going directly into the selamlık, Kamil went first to the harem to find Jamila. He was told that she was in the nursery. When Kamil reached the nursery, Jamila was talking with an experienced kalfa who she had just assigned as the baby's dadı. The servant was putting the baby to sleep. Jamila stepped out of the nursery so as not to disturb the baby.

"Jamila, I thought the baby was supposed to be born several weeks later," said Kamil. "Tell me everything that has happened."

Jamila led Kamil to a room where they could talk privately and gestured for him to have a seat. Then she told him the details of the night before from the time she was awoken by Ziya's knock on the door until the present moment.

"Jamila, this is my fault. I should have been here last night."

"This is God's will, Kamil Efendi. Don't blame yourself. You could not prevent a death that has been ordained by God. But if you had been here and tried your best to prevent it, at least your conscience would be clear now...," Jamila said in a neutral tone of voice.

"I will never forgive myself for not being here," Kamil replied. "How is Ziya taking it?"

"Ziya is in great anguish. As you know, he loved Nilufer very much," replied Jamila. "Why don't you go to his side now? I'm sure he is in great need of your support."

With his head bowed low, Kamil started walking towards the main hall of the selamlık where Ziya was accepting condolences from male friends, neighbors and relatives.

Jamila went to Nilufer's bedroom. She could hardly believe that the room which just a year ago housed Nilufer's bridal throne now held her death bed. Both the bedroom and the adjacent sitting room were filled with women who had come to pay their last respects to Nilufer and to give condolences to the grief-stricken families.

The women were all weeping, but there was no wailing – just quiet acceptance of an irrevocable fate. Two young *hafiz** girls had been called in to continuously recite the Quran at Nilufer's bedside.

As news of Nilufer's death spread, a constant stream of visitors came and went. Palace dignitaries and their wives, officials from the Ottoman elite, relatives, family friends and neighbors –rich and poor alike- poured into the Beylerbeyi mansion to give their condolences and comfort to the bereaved families. They all brought food, which, in turn, was served, to the mourners. The old Turkish adage, "Sharing increases joy and decreases sorrow," was once more tested and found to be true. Jamila was deeply grateful for this outpouring of support in their time of need.

The visitors all left after the evening prayer. Everyone in the mansion was still in a state of shock. The funeral was to be held the next day after the noon prayer, so all needed to get some rest. Kamil Efendi went to bed in the adjacent bedroom as he frequently did of late. After checking on the baby and giving Ziya some herbal medicine that would help him sleep, Jamila retired for the night.

The intense activities during the day had absorbed Jamila's attention and prevented her from facing their loss. But now that she was alone, the dimensions of that loss became all too clear: Ziya had lost his wife, his partner, his beloved… The baby had lost its mother, the most precious asset any baby can have… And Jamila had lost a dearly loved daughter… She felt overwhelmed. How would they make it through the next day and all the days to follow? Jamila knew there was only one answer to that question: by the grace of God. She prayed fervently that God give her and her family the strength and fortitude to bear this heavy trial.

Jamila was exhausted and she soon fell into a deep sleep. Shortly before dawn she suddenly woke up. Jamila had seen Nilufer in her dream: She saw herself riding in a white carriage drawn by four white horses. Jamila was going to Nilufer's funeral. She traveled

* One who has committed the Quran to memory.

for some time on a tree-lined road. Then the carriage turned off the main road to a narrow lane. On both sides of the lane there were fields of flowers for as far as Jamila could see. The flowers were of every imaginable color and they were more beautiful than any flowers she had ever seen on earth. Jamila was enchanted by the flowers! She stopped the carriage, got out and started walking among them. She bent down and picked several; they gave off an intoxicating fragrance. Jamila was so enraptured by the flowers that she sat down in the field and forgot that she was supposed to go to the funeral. Suddenly Nilufer appeared next to Jamila. She was wearing a white dress and a white head cover, and she looked lovelier than ever. Her face was illuminated with light. Nilufer sat down next to Jamila without saying a word. She only smiled... It was a smile of sweet contentment.

Then Jamila woke up. The fragrance of the flowers lingered on a moment. Jamila had an intense feeling of serenity, as if everything was just as it should be. Nilufer was all right; she had simply passed to another plane of existence. There was nothing to worry about...

Jamila got up and went to Ziya's room. She found Ziya sitting on a prayer rug.

"Ziya!" Jamila exclaimed. "I've seen Nilufer in a dream. She was smiling, Ziya. So she must be alright."

Startled, Ziya looked up at his mother. "Why do you say that, Anneciğim? Tell me what you saw."

Jamila vividly described her dream to her son; the fields, the flowers, Nilufer's smile. And then she told him about the serenity she felt when she woke up.

"Ziya, it must be a sign for us that Nilufer is all right," Jamila said, fully convinced of the truth of her words.

"I need to believe that, Anne," responded Ziya.

Jamila knelt down and put her arms around Ziya as she had done so many times in the past when her son needed comforting.

"Ziya, we know that good dreams are from God," said Jamila. "This was a beautiful dream. It was no coincidence. You must believe that Nilufer is all right."

Ziya slowly nodded his head. The strained look on his face softened a little as the heavy feeling in his chest lightened up.

"This is what life is all about, isn't it, Anne? Getting prepared for the day when all preparation ends."

"Yes, my son; that is what life is all about. But we tend to forget that simple truth so easily. We get caught up in the hustle and bustle of daily life; our needs and desires and difficulties all veil that simple truth from us."

Ziya looked his mother in the eyes and said, "Anne, if I ever forget again, please remind me, because that is the only thing that gives meaning to Nilufer's death."

Jamila slowly got up to return to her room. Today they had a very difficult task before them, they had to bury Nilufer. But somehow Jamila felt in her heart that they would get through this ordeal and that they would be the wiser for it.

After Jamila got dressed, she went directly to the nursery to see how the new baby girl was doing. The baby's wet-nurse had just fed her and she was sleeping contentedly in her cradle. Jamila looked at the baby carefully. She was so small and vulnerable, but she would have to become a strong girl to overcome this blow dealt to her by fate.

Jamila left the baby with its dadı and went to see about funeral arrangements. A convoy of carriages had already begun to form in front of the mansion. Friends and relatives from far and near were gathering to perform their final duty for Nilufer, whose body was to be taken to the Beylerbeyi Mosque and later buried in the Beylerbeyi cemetery. As the time of the noon prayer approached, the convoy set out for the mosque. It was headed by the carriage of Nilufer's family. All the women remained in their carriages as the imam led the men in the noon prayer followed by the funeral prayer. It was a simple, but solemn ceremony. After the prayer, Nilufer's coffin was placed in an ox-drawn funeral cart and the funeral procession started up the hill to the cemetery. With some strenuous effort on the part of the horses and oxen, the funeral procession arrived at the graveyard.

High on a hill, the cemetery commanded a panoramic view of the Bosphorus Straits. Again the women remained in the carriages while the imam read the Quran and prayed at Nilufer's gravesite as her body was lowered into the grave. There was a gentle breeze blowing from the Straits. Jamila looked around at the peaceful cemetery. Dignified carved headstones intermingled haphazardly with cypress trees and wildflowers as if to show that death is a natural part of life. The only signs of sorrow visible to Jamila were the drooping branches of the weeping willow trees and the tears streaming down her own face as the last shovel of dirt was tossed onto Nilufer's grave. Then the convoy headed down the hill again.

All afternoon the house was filled with a constant flow of visitors conveying their condolences to the bereaved families. It was a dignified communal sharing of grief. Hodjas came to chant appropriate verses of the Quran and to make prayers for Nilufer's salvation. Solemn hymns were sung regarding death.

In the evening, after all the visitors and hodjas had left, Jamila, Kamil and Ziya went together to the nursery to see the baby.

"Ziya, are you aware that we haven't yet given the baby a name?" asked Jamila.

"I am, Anneciğim, but my mind has been so absorbed that I haven't had a chance to think about names. Do you have any suggestions?" asked Ziya.

"What about Kadriye? It's a powerful name; it should give strength to our little girl," replied Jamila.

"What do you think, Baba?" Ziya asked Kamil Efendi.

"I think it's a very appropriate name," Kamil replied.

Ziya picked his daughter up and after making the call to prayer in her right ear, he pronounced her new name, Kadriye.

The stream of visitors conveying their condolences continued for the next two weeks. Their concern helped ease the pain of Jamila and her family, and their support helped them all to adjust to this harsh, new reality.

The one source of joy in Jamila's life was baby Kadriye. Unaware of the tragedy that had befallen her, the baby thrived on both the milk and the attention she received. She was like a shining star in the midst of darkness, bringing a smile to the lips of those around her who were otherwise immersed in grief.

The first months after Kadriye's birth and Nilufer's death were spent in deep reflection and endless discussion about life and death. Jamila and Ziya spent almost every evening discussing these topics, trying to break through heavy veils of thought to get to essential truths. What was the real purpose of life? Had Nilufer achieved this purpose? At what point were Jamila and Ziya in their life journeys? What lessons could they learn from Nilufer's death? Jamila and Ziya often talked until the early hours of the morning. It was not only a time of soul-searching, but a period of psychological therapy as well, especially for Ziya. Talking about Nilufer's death seemed to be the only means to calm down the thoughts and emotions welling up in Ziya's mind and heart, the only way to ease the agonizing pain Ziya felt.

"Anneciğim, Nilufer died so young. She was just at the beginning of her adult life. Kadriye has been left without her mother. Sometimes I can't make any sense out of it," Ziya said with a confused look on his face.

"Ziya, sometimes things don't appear as they really are," Jamila responded. "Do you remember I once told you the story about a good man walking in the desert who was killed by a lion? That appears to be an act of injustice to such a good person. However, he had prayed to God for a high station in heaven, but his works in this life were not enough to warrant that high position. So God gave him a cruel death and made him a martyr, which enabled him to attain the high station he had prayed for."

"Anne, are you suggesting that Nilufer is a martyr?" Ziya asked in astonishment.

"Yes, Ziya, women who die in childbirth are considered to be martyrs in our religion. Perhaps Nilufer's good works in her short lifetime were not enough to give her a high station in the afterlife. But as a martyr, she will have that high station. Also, my son, did you ever think that maybe we don't have enough good works to attain the station we want in the next world, but that if we accept this trial with patience, it might be a vehicle to carry us to a higher station?"

"No, Anneciğim, I never thought about it like that. Are you saying that some good for all of us can come out of Nilufer's death?"

"Ziya, that depends on how you perceive death. Don't the dervishes say, *Mevla neylerse güzel eyler.**

As the weeks and months passed, Jamila tried to turn her attention more and more to Kadriye, and she encouraged Ziya to do the same. Jamila was determined to give Kadriye as normal a life as possible, so eight months later when the baby's first tooth appeared, Jamila invited her close friends and relatives to a traditional dinner called the *diş buğdayı*. In addition to a regular meal, a dish made from sweetened wheat (*buğday*), dried fruit and nuts was served. All the guests brought a gift for the baby in celebration of the new tooth.

Among the guests was Rabia, Jamila's childhood friend. Their friendship had endured over the years and, like vintage wine, it had mellowed with time. Rabia waited for all the other guests to leave. She had an anxious look on her face. Jamila understood that Rabia had something she wanted to talk about privately, but she had no idea what it was.

"Rabia, what's troubling you? Is there anything I can do to help?" Jamila asked with concern.

"My dear sister," Rabia replied with a compassionate tone of voice, "I wish with all my heart that I were not the one to bring you this news."

"What is it, Rabia? You know you can confide in me," said Jamila. "Has someone hurt or harmed you in some way? Please tell me what has happened."

"No, my dear Jamila, I have not been wronged," answered Rabia. "It's you…"

"Me?" Jamila asked with astonishment. "What do you mean?"

"Jamila, yesterday I went to visit my cousin Refia in Sariyer. She had also invited some women from the surrounding areas for tea. Among them was a young woman, Bedrifelek Hanım, who has been living with her husband in Rumeli Kavagi for more than a year. She complained that because of her husband's work, he was not able to spend much time at home. When I asked Bedrifelek Hanım who her husband was, she replied that her husband was assistant chief physician at the palace –Kamil Efendi..."

Jamila's face turned chalk white. In a hushed voice, she said, "Go on…"

Rabia continued, "She is a former Georgian slave girl from the harem of the Sultan's sister, Esma Sultan. That's all I know about her, Jamila, except that she is expecting a baby in three months."

"Rabia, there must be some kind of mistake here. Kamil wouldn't do such a thing. I'll go there first thing tomorrow morning to see for myself," said Jamila.

"I won't allow you to go alone; I'll be here early tomorrow morning and we'll go together," Rabia responded. She hugged Jamila tightly and then took her leave.

Jamila waited for Kamil to come home, but he sent a message that he would be staying at the palace all night...

She didn't want to say anything to Ziya about what Rabia had told her until she had seen the situation for herself. So after telling Ziya about the dinner for Kadriye's first tooth, she excused herself, saying that she had a bad headache.

Jamila went to bed early, but she could not sleep. She kept turning over in her mind what Rabia had told her. Was it possible that Kamil had a second wife? He had never once indicated to Jamila that he wanted to marry again. To her knowledge, Kamil had never shown interest in any other woman. There must be some explanation for this. On the other hand, there was only one assistant head physician at the palace named Kamil Efendi... Jamila didn't know what to think.

After a night of troubled sleep, Jamila was up before dawn the next morning. First she performed the ritual morning prayer, and then she prayed fervently for guidance and protection for herself and her family. Shortly after sunrise, Rabia arrived. The women had a quick breakfast and then went down the stairs to the private dock. The foreman tried to discourage Jamila from setting out in the caique because of the rough weather, but Jamila was determined to go to Rumeli Kavagi. Dark clouds were gathering over the Straits and a strong wind rocked the small boat. The oarsmen had difficulty navigating the light craft in the turbulent waters. After a long and treacherous journey, the caique finally crossed the Straits and arrived at Rumeli Kavagi in mid-morning. Jamila instructed the foreman to wait at the dock with the oarsmen while she and Rabia Hanım paid a visit.

Rumeli Kavagi was the farthest settlement on the Straits before the mouth of the Black Sea. Because it was sparsely inhabited, Jamila and Rabia had no difficulty in locating the house where Bedrifelek Hanım and her husband lived. It appeared to be the largest house in the small settlement.

The women knocked on the door and a servant showed them into a sitting room in the harem. She did not ask who they were. As Jamila walked into the room, she noticed a framed photograph sitting on a console. Suddenly Jamila felt as if her breath had been knocked out of her. It was a picture of Kamil and a young woman, apparently Bedrifelek Hanım. Trying not to collapse, she clung to Rabia's arm. Rabia led her to the closest chair. Taking a small bottle of cologne from her bag, Rabia rubbed it on Jamila's forehead and wrists. The servant returned to inform them that Bedrifelek Hanım was indisposed, but that Kamil Efendi would be coming shortly. Rabia asked the servant to bring some water.

The water had a calming effect on Jamila, but she felt as if her vital energy had been depleted, as if she had been crushed under a heavy weight. Rabia held Jamila's hand tightly.

Before long, Kamil Efendi appeared. As he walked into the room, he froze in his tracks and his face turned pale. Kamil was obviously astonished to find Jamila in front of him.

"Jamila, what are you doing here?" Kamil asked in a strained tone of voice. "How did you find your way?"

Ignoring his question, Jamila asked, "Can we speak privately for a few minutes?"

"Yes, of course," Kamil replied soberly, "this way."

Jamila followed Kamil into an adjacent room. It appeared to be Kamil's study. After taking a seat, Jamila said:

"Kamil Efendi, I think I deserve an explanation. Why haven't you told me about this before?"

"Jamila," responded Kamil, "I didn't know how to tell you. I didn't want to hurt you."

"Do you love her?" Jamila asked.

"I didn't marry Bedrifelek Hanım for love. I married her because of her close connections with the Sultan. She was raised in the harem of the Sultan's favorite sister, Esma Sultan. Jamila, you know how my lack of professional advancement has tortured me. I thought my marriage with Bedrifelek would secure my advancement."

"Has it?" Jamila asked.

"Not yet, but I have the word of Esma Sultan that when the current chief physician's term is ended, she will recommend me to her brother, the Sultan," replied Kamil.

"I see," said Jamila. "I came here, Kamil, to learn if you have put your own interests before the best interests of our family. Now that I know you have, I would like to leave."

"Jamila..." said Kamil.

Not allowing Kamil to finish his sentence, Jamila got up, went to the next room and left with Rabia.

Rabia did not have to ask Jamila how she was. She understood from the look on her face that Jamila was devastated. They returned to the caique as quickly as possible and started to cross the Straits again. There was still a strong wind and rough waves. Heavy dark clouds hung ominously overhead. When the small craft reached mid-point between the two shores, rain suddenly began to pour down. The umbrellas that the women held over their heads were utterly useless. Everyone became soaked from head to toe. Only with extraordinary effort were the oarsmen able to take the caique back to the Beylerbeyi mansion dock.

Once inside, the women immediately changed their clothes. Jamila was exhausted, and Rabia instructed the servants to give her some hot tea and put her to bed. She said she would check in on Jamila the next day.

That evening when Ziya came home from work, he found his mother in bed with a burning fever. Unaware of the events that had transpired that day, Ziya sent a message to his father to come home as quickly as possible. Efforts of the servants to reduce the fever with cold compresses had no success whatsoever. When Kamil arrived, he gave Jamila medicine, but the fever continued to rage. Jamila was close to delirium. She did not know where she was nor did she recognize anyone. She appeared to be in a state of limbo somewhere between sleep and consciousness. Nightmares stalked her. Strange creatures came and went in a surrealistic world. She relived her encounter with Kamil at Rumeli Kavagi again and again. Jamila tried to wake up, but she couldn't...

Chapter 9

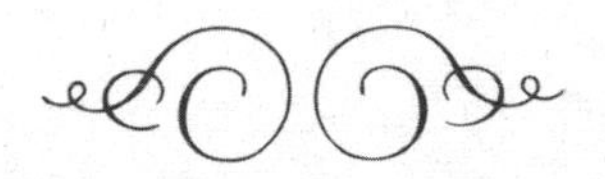

Beylerbeyi

The fever persisted for forty-eight hours before it finally broke. When Jamila woke up, Rabia and Gulshah Dadı were at her side.

"Jamila, thank God you are alright. You gave us a tremendous scare," said Rabia.

"I don't remember anything," Jamila said with a weak voice. "How long have I been in bed?"

"You had a burning fever, Jamila. It lasted forty-eight hours," replied Rabia.

Jamila was astonished to learn that she had been in bed for two days. Then she recalled the events leading up to her fever –the hazardous trip to Rumeli Kavagi, her conversation with Kamil, and the deluge of rain on the way back… Jamila felt extremely tired. Her face was very pale. She asked Gulshah Dadı for some water, but she refused to eat anything. She just wanted to sleep…

After that Jamila spent days on end in bed, mostly sleeping. She ate just enough to stay alive. Ziya was extremely concerned about his mother. When he asked his father about the cause of his mother's condition, Kamil Efendi explained to Ziya what had happened. Now it was Ziya's turn to support his mother in her time of pain. Every night when Ziya came home from work, he went to his mother's side to comfort her. He never left her alone. Frequently he brought little Kadriye into her room, hoping that she might cheer Jamila up.

Days and weeks passed, but Jamila was unable to get up and around. She felt as if she had lost her life energy, and she did not know how to get it back. Ziya, Kamil Efendi, Gulshah Dadı, Rabia, Zainab Hanım and many others tried in vain to coax Jamila back to normal life.

In her heart Jamila was searching for a way to resolve her relationship with Kamil. It appeared that Jamila's only options were either to accept Kamil's marriage to Bedrifelek Hanım or divorce him. However, neither option was acceptable to Jamila. She had devoted all of her adult life to this marriage, and she could not imagine any other life for herself. Furthermore, Jamila was still deeply in love with Kamil. She was afraid of losing his love. Although the last several years of their relationship had been very unfulfilling for Jamila, still she had the hope that one day their marriage would return to normal. Jamila was very confused. She didn't know what to do, so she did nothing … except sleep.

Then one night six weeks after Jamila had gone to bed with a fever, she had a dream. She saw Husnu Baba, the sheik who had been her father's childhood friend. Husnu Baba was sitting cross-legged on a sheepskin rug in his dervish hall. The fragrance of roses filled the room. He was dressed in a long white robe, and he had a pointed green dervish cap on his head with a white turban wrapped around it. A single red rose was tucked into his turban. He had smiling blue eyes and a snow-white beard. A vortex of light was rising behind him.

"Jamila *kızım*,* seek love from its source, not its channel," he said in a compassionate tone of voice.

Jamila woke up the next morning before dawn. She recalled Husnu Baba's words: "seek love from its source, not its channel." What did the sheik mean? What was the source of love and what was its channel? Jamila thought long and hard about Husnu Baba's words throughout the day. Slowly she began to comprehend exactly what he meant.

---

* "my daughter"

Jamila understood that Husnu Baba was telling her to seek love from God, the source of all love. Human beings are only channels of God's love. Kamil had been a channel for God's love for many years, but now that channel was blocked by Kamil's own self-interest. Jamila no longer felt afraid of losing Kamil. Now she understood that losing Kamil did not mean losing love. He was just one of many channels of love in her life.

Jamila felt a tremendous emotional relief. Now she knew what she had to do. She got out of bed and called Gulshah Dadı. She asked the elderly woman if Kamil Efendi had come home yet. The dadı said that he was in the next room, so Jamila asked her to call him. Kamil entered the room with a look of surprise on his face.

"Jamila, how wonderful. You're on your feet again," he said excitedly.

"Yes, Kamil, thank God, I am back on my feet," Jamila replied. "I asked Gulshah Dadı to call you because we need to discuss a serious matter – the terms for our divorce. If you recall, the stipulation was put in our marriage contract that if you took a second wife, we would become divorced. I hope we can divorce with the least amount of discomfort for all of us."

Kamil was obviously shaken my Jamila's words. The conviction in her voice, however, told him that the decision she had made was irrevocable. Kamil looked confused and hurt, as if he had not anticipated this kind of decision from Jamila.

"I had hoped that things would not end this way," Kamil responded. "Are you sure this is what you want?"

"This is not what I want, Kamil, but it is what I have to do. You have left me no other acceptable choice," replied Jamila.

As he opened the door to leave the room, Kamil said quietly, "We can come to an agreement about divorce terms this evening when Ziya comes home from work."

Jamila felt intensely serene. She didn't know which direction her life would take after her divorce, but she felt secure in God's hands. Wasn't the dream proof that God would guide her? Her only purpose now was to draw closer and closer to the source of love.

That evening after Ziya came home, Jamila told him about her decision. Ziya was naturally upset that his parents were divorcing, but he understood his mother's pain. When Kamil Efendi came home, they sat down together and discussed arrangements for the future. Kamil had planned to leave the Beylerbeyi house to Ziya anyway after his death, so they decided that the rights to half of the mansion would be turned over to Ziya immediately and the other half would be given to Jamila in lieu of her delayed mahr payment. Upon her death Jamila's share of the house would go to Ziya. Kamil would move the rest of his personal belongings to his house in Rumeli Kavagi.

As soon as their discussion ended, Jamila went to bed because she had something very important she wanted to do the next day.

Early the next morning Jamila got up and got dressed. She felt much better than she had for weeks. Informing the foreman that she had some business to attend to, she asked him to prepare the carriage. After having breakfast and spending close to an hour with Kadriye, Jamila put on her ferace and veil. Then she stepped outside and got into the carriage waiting at the gate. She told the driver to head towards Kanlica.

As they drove along the coastal road, Jamila drew back the curtain and looked out at the Straits. It was a beautiful sunny day and the rays of the sun sparkled like diamonds on the calm water. Dozens of small fishing craft bobbed up and down on the water's surface as scores of seagulls squawked overhead. Seeing the teeming life on the Straits, Jamila, too, felt new life flowing in her veins.

When the carriage turned from the coastal road onto the main street in Kanlica, a flood of memories inundated Jamila's mind. The first stage of her life had passed here in the warm embrace of her family and childhood friends. Then her life in Beylerbeyi had comprised a second stage with her new family. Now Jamila felt that she was at the threshold of yet another stage in life, and it pleased her that this stage would begin in Kanlica.

The driver pulled the carriage over to the side of the road and got down.

"Where precisely would you like to go, Hanım Efendi?" he asked.

"Take me to the *tekke* of Husnu Baba."

They drove for another ten minutes and then the driver turned off the street to a narrow lane. At the end of the lane stood a large rambling wooden building. It was situated in an orchard that contained countless numbers of different fruit trees – apple, pear, pomegranate, peach, plum, quince and many more. Behind the house there was a vegetable garden that extended as far as the eye could see. There were also flowers, especially roses, popping up out of every empty space. All in all, it was a picture of abundance itself.

Jamila got out of the carriage and slowly crossed a stone path that led to the front door. A mother cat and her four kittens were curled up at the side of the door. The kittens were all busy nursing. The mother cat glanced up at Jamila as she knocked on the door but, feeling no threat, she turned her attention back to her kittens. A young man wearing baggy clothing and a skullcap opened the door. Jamila said she had come to see Husnu Baba. The young man showed her to a small room near the entrance and asked her to wait. Then he disappeared. Returning a few minutes later, he asked Jamila to follow him. The young man took Jamila to a large hall where the sheik was waiting for her.

Husnu Baba was sitting on a sheepskin in a corner of the large room just as he had been in Jamila's dream. He was also dressed in the same white robe and green dervish hat. There was even a rose tucked in the turban wrapped around his hat.

"Welcome, Jamila *kızım*," he said as if he had been expecting her. Jamila was surprised that the sheik knew her name because she had not seen him since she was a child.

"Husnu Baba, I am the daughter of your old friend Hikmet Bey..." Jamila said.

"Yes, of course," replied Husnu Baba. "Your father and I spent a lot of time together when we were children. I was deeply saddened to learn about the death of your parents. May God have mercy on their souls."

"In the past several years I have been faced with other trials as well..." began Jamila.

"Let me tell you one of Rumi's stories *kızım*," Husnu Baba said.

"In olden times there was a king who was wealthy in both worldly goods and spirit. He was going to hunt one day with his courtiers when he saw a handmaiden on the king's highway. The king's soul became enthralled by the young woman, so he bought her. After he fulfilled his desire, the handmaiden became sick.

"The king gathered all his physicians together and told them that he would give his treasure to whoever could heal the girl. The physicians were arrogant and said that they had a medicine for every cure, but they were unable to heal her. Devastated, the king ran to the mosque and raised a cry of supplication from the depths of his soul. In the midst of weeping, he fell asleep and saw an old man in his dream. The old man told him that his prayer had been accepted and that a stranger would arrive the next day. He said that the king should trust him for he was a skillful physician.

"The next day the king watched for the skillful physician. When he saw him approaching, he went to meet the traveler himself. After the king welcomed the physician, he told him about the girl's sickness and took him to her bedside. The physician observed the color of her face and he took her pulse. And he understood that she was sick in heart, not in body.

"The physician asked the king to make everyone leave the palace so that he could be alone with the girl to ask her some questions. The king did as he was asked, and the physician began questioning the girl about her family and her work. He watched the girl's face and kept his finger on her pulse. They discussed many details about the girl's past, the places she worked and her former owners. She gave no sign until the physician mentioned Samarcand. Then her face turned red and her pulse began to throb, because the girl had been parted from a goldsmith from Samarcand.

"The physician told the girl not to worry for he would take care of everything. Then he went to the king and told him the situation. He also told him to send for the goldsmith and tempt him with gold and robes of honor.

"The king sent two messengers to the Samarcand goldsmith with gold and silver and robes of honor. They told him the king had chosen him as his personal goldsmith. When the goldsmith saw all that wealth, he agreed to leave his town and family and return with them. The king welcomed the goldsmith and wed the handmaiden to him. He allowed them to be happy together for six months until the girl's health was restored.

"Then the physician gave the goldsmith a potion that slowly undermined his health. He became ugly and sallow-cheeked, and little by little the girl turned away from him. By the time he died, the handmaiden had been cured of her love for him. Then she was finally able to love the Living King."*

As Jamila was thinking about the meaning of the story, she heard the call to prayer. Excusing herself so that Husnu Baba could lead the dervishes in prayer, Jamila said she would come again soon. Husnu Baba nodded his head and Jamila left.

All the way home Jamila thought about the story and why Husnu Baba had told her that particular tale. Slowly Jamila understood that just as the handmaiden had loved the goldsmith instead of the King (representing God), she, too, had put her love for Kamil before her love for God. But now because of his selfishness, Kamil was no longer pleasing to Jamila's eyes. Now she, too, was ready to put the Living King first in her life. As the carriage proceeded

---

* Paraphrased from Jalaluddin Rumi's *Mathnawi*, Bk. I.

towards Beylerbeyi along the narrow coastal road, Jamila's heart was filled with peace.

That evening Jamila told Ziya about her visit to Husnu Baba and the tekke. She repeated to him the story about the King and the Handmaiden. And she also told him about her newly-found peace. Ziya was intrigued by it all because he could see that a glow of light was returning to his mother's face. So he told Jamila that he would like to accompany her on her next visit to Husnu Baba.

A week later Jamila and Ziya went together to the tekke. Jamila was very pleased that Ziya was accompanying her because at times he still had difficulty accepting Nilufer's death. Jamila was anxious for Kadriye to have a new mother, but she felt it would be wrong to open the subject of remarriage to Ziya before he had come to terms with his former wife's death.

When they arrived at the dervish lodge, Jamila and Ziya had to wait for some time because a large group of Uzbek pilgrims had arrived on their way to Mecca. They wanted to get Husnu Baba's blessing before they continued on their journey. While the pilgrims were busy eating the plentiful meal that had been prepared for them, Husnu Baba called Jamila and Ziya into his private study.

The sheik looked at Ziya carefully and then said smilingly:

"Jamila *kızım*, you have a son with a heart of gold; it's a pity you didn't give birth to ten more children like him."

Jamila smiled in return. "Yes, Ziya is pure gold, but his heart was deeply wounded by the death of his wife a year ago."

Husnu Baba turned to Ziya: "My son, life is like a river. If you flow with it, your heart will be at ease. If you try and struggle against it, you will only find disappointment and despair. Resistance to God's plan is the cause of all difficulties and illnesses. Surrender to His plan is the key to peace and serenity."

The sheik's words rang true for Ziya. Although he had not been aware of it, Ziya had been resisting God's plan. He did not want to accept Nilufer's death but, on the other hand, he could do nothing to change it. He had become caught up on her death, unable to move forward in life.

Husnu Baba's words had been addressed to Ziya, but Jamila took them to heart as well. Hadn't she been struggling against the flow of life in her relationship with Kamil? Hadn't she tried to freeze in time the good years of their marriage? Her efforts had only caused her pain and unhappiness. Now she was more certain than ever that she had made the right decision to divorce Kamil. Holding on to a relationship where there was no longer trust and respect would only mean more heartbreak for Jamila.

A knock on the door interrupted the short visit. The Uzbek pilgrims were asking for Husnu Baba to make a prayer at the end of the meal. Jamila and Ziya excused themselves and promised to return soon. As they left the dervish lodge, Jamila could see that Ziya's heart was more peaceful; it was reflected in his face.

Jamila and Ziya continued visiting the dervish lodge on a regular basis. Husnu Baba gave talks every Friday afternoon, and Jamila and Ziya were careful not to miss them. Husnu Baba's profound words of wisdom were like salve to the wounded hearts of Jamila and Ziya. The sheik was truly a healer of souls. Through the insights they gained from Husnu Baba's talks, Jamila and Ziya were able to look at life from a new perspective – a cosmic perspective.

Jamila no longer saw her marriage as the center of her world as she had for so many years. Now God's plan was her center; all her efforts were focused on trying to understand and find her role in that plan.

Jamila's life took on new direction and meaning. She became more active in helping others less fortunate than herself. She had inherited several shops and some farmland from her parents, along with their house and other property. Setting up a waqf* for orphans, she began to use the income from her property to cover

---

* Pious foundation established by individual men or women.

educational expenses for poor orphans. The smiles on the faces of these children gave Jamila a tremendous sense of satisfaction. Giving to others with no expectations of anything in return -except the approval of God- brought with it its own special reward. Ziya, too, became involved in waqf activities and through his efforts the scope of the program for orphans increased several fold. Helping others was just the medicine they needed to heal their own hearts.

Life had become purposeful and rewarding again. The only thing missing was a mother for Kadriye who was now two and a half years-old. Jamila had opened the topic once, but all Ziya had said was "maybe sometime." In spite of Ziya's lack of interest in remarriage, Jamila kept her eye open for prospective candidates, but none of the young women she knew seemed mature enough for Ziya. He had been put through a test of fire and it would not be easy to find a young woman who could truly understand and appreciate what he had suffered.

Jamila and Ziya continued to attend Husnu Baba's talks every Friday. Jamila listened to them from behind a wooden lattice balcony overlooking the main hall along with the rest of the women. Since it was usually quite crowded, Jamila liked to come early so she could sit close to the front in order to hear the talk clearly. One Friday afternoon before it became crowded, Jamila noticed a young woman she had never seen before. There was something special about her. After taking another careful look, Jamila realized that it was the light in her face that she was attracted by. The balcony was rapidly filling up and the talk was about to begin. So Jamila decided to introduce herself to the young woman after the talk.

Husnu Baba spoke on the topic of *insan-ı kamil* or the perfected human being. Saying that becoming a perfected human being was the goal of this journey in life, the sheik talked about how this goal can be reached. He said that it was basically all about balancing the heart and the mind. When the mind dominates a person's inner world, he can justify any act and can become cruel and oppressive. On the other hand, when the heart dominates, a person can become too soft and submissive. But when the heart and mind are in balance, the heart prevents oppression and the mind prevents servility. Consequently, justice can reign. Husnu Baba went on to say that, another example of balance between the heart and mind was love with wisdom. Without wisdom, love can often be blind. But when love is balanced with wisdom, we neither hurt others nor allow others to hurt us, and again justice is allowed to reign.

Jamila carefully followed Husnu Baba's words. When she applied these truths to her own life, she realized that she had not loved with wisdom. She had loved Kamil blindly and had been profoundly hurt by him in the end. If only she had learned these truths earlier. But, on the other hand, she was grateful to be learning them now. Some people never learn them.

As soon as Husnu Baba's talk was finished, Jamila looked around to see if she could locate the young woman, she had seen earlier. With difficulty she made her way through the crowd to the place where the young woman had been sitting. But to Jamila's disappointment, she was gone.

Jamila's activities related to the orphanage began taking up more and more of her time. She wanted to do all she could for others in the remainder of her life. Jamila had convinced many of her friends to become involved in the project, and the number of orphans they could help was rapidly increasing. As usual, Rabia was the hardest worker of all the volunteers. She frequently gave large dinners in her home for women from the Ottoman elite, all of whom made contributions to the waqf. Rabia was an excellent organizer. She not only provided exquisite cuisine, but she arranged musical programs for the women as well and, as a result, her dinners were quite popular.

Today Rabia was giving another dinner, but unfortunately, Jamila was running late. She had lost track of time while playing with Kadriye, and now she had to rush. Hurrying to her carriage, Jamila asked the driver to take her to Rabia Hanım's house in

Kanlica as quickly as possible. Once she arrived, Jamila rushed into the mansion. As she went up the stairs she heard the sound of music; the program had already begun.

The large hall was full of women, so Jamila took a place at the back of the room close to the door. She could not see who was playing the piano, but the music was exquisite. Jamila had never heard the piano played with such sensitivity and beauty. It was as if the pianist were striking chords in Jamila's soul. No one made a sound. All were enraptured by the captivating sound of the music. When the recital was over, the women all stood up and applauded for a long time. Jamila's eyes were searching for Rabia. As she made her way among the crowd, Jamila saw her friend standing next to the piano. Rabia motioned for Jamila to come there.

When Jamila arrived to where her friend was standing, Rabia said she wanted to introduce Jamila to the pianist. The young woman stood up and turned around towards Jamila.

"Jamila, please meet our wonderfully accomplished pianist, Didenur Hanım," Rabia said.

Jamila was astounded. She did not know what to say. The pianist was the young woman she had seen at the tekke…

After staring at Didenur with amazement, Jamila replied: "Oh… excuse me… I'm very pleased to meet you. Your music is marvelous."

"How kind you are," responded Didenur. "I'm so glad you like my music."

Didenur was besieged by women congratulating her on her performance. Most of the crowd had gravitated towards her. Jamila signaled for Rabia to follow her to the next room.

"Rabia, who is Didenur Hanım? What do you know about her? How did you find her? Tell me everything," Jamila said excitedly.

Rabia smiled at Jamila's enthusiasm. She understood that there was more to her friend's questions than just an appreciation of music.

"I met her at Princess Aliye's palace. She appears to have been living there for some time. She is a *saraylı* who was in the service of Aliye Sultan when she was a young princess. Didenur Hanım was formerly married to an army colonel, but they divorced several years ago. When I heard her play the piano, I was mezmerized by it. So I immediately invited her here."

"Does she have any children from her first marriage?" Jamila asked.

"Not that I know of, my dear sister. Why do you ask?" Rabia inquired.

"I'm not sure, but the first time I saw her I felt there was something very special about her. Today after listening to her play, I feel even stronger about it. What do you think, Rabia?"

"You're right, Jamila. She has a lot of light. You can see it in her face and feel it in her music..." replied Rabia.

Their conversation was interrupted by a number of women coming into the room. It was time for dinner, so both Rabia and Jamila needed to attend to the guests. Rabia instructed her servants to set up the dinner trays as quickly as possible. The experienced and skillful servants quickly turned what was previously a recital hall into an elegant dining room. After the guests were all seated comfortably, Rabia called for the food to be brought in. One culinary delight followed another with short intervals in between.

After all the women had eaten their fill and the last dish was removed by the servants, the coffee service began. While the guests were sipping their coffee, Rabia thanked everyone for coming and introduced Jamila to make a short speech. Jamila began telling the women about the waqf for orphans and the work that the waqf had been doing.

"With your support the work of the waqf has grown by leaps and bounds," Jamila said. "We started out providing the educational expenses of ten orphans, but now we are about to begin building a permanent facility that will house fifty orphans. The land is ready and my son has completed the architectural design for the building. If we get your continued support, we can begin construction soon. As we all know, giving support to orphans is a highly laudable act. I would like to thank you in advance for your generosity and kindness."

Two large baskets were placed at the door of the hall for donations as the guests left. At the end of the day they were both brimming with gold coins.

That evening Jamila eagerly awaited Ziya's return. She had some important things to discuss with him. Jamila was in the nursery playing with Kadriye when Ziya arrived. He understood from the broad smile on his mother's face that she had had a good day. Giving Kadriye a kiss on the forehead, Ziya turned to his mother:

"Anneciğim, does your smile tell me that we can immediately begin building the orphanage?" Ziya asked.

"Indeed, it does," replied Jamila. "Thank God, the dinner went well. The women contributed generously, my son. You can begin building at once."

"I'm proud of you, Anne. This orphanage was just a dream a year ago," Ziya commented.

"Yes, Ziya, it was just a dream. But the key here is not just to be able to dream, but to dream what is pleasing to God. Then everything becomes easy, easier than one can ever imagine."

"How can I doubt that, Anneciğim? I am seeing your dream unfold in front of my eyes," Ziya said smilingly.

"Ziya," continued Jamila, "Something else happened today. When I arrived at Rabia's home, the piano recital had already begun. It was the most beautiful music I have ever heard. I was truly enchanted. After the recital ended, Rabia introduced me to the pianist, Didenur Hanım. To my amazement, it was the young woman I mentioned to you that I had seen at the tekke. I knew from the moment I first saw her that there was something special about her, and today my first impression was further confirmed. She has a beautiful aura of light. I can see it in her face, as well. Ziya, I want you to meet her."

"Anne, I'm sure she is a very fine person, but you know I am not looking for a wife," Ziya replied disinterestedly.

"Ziya, you may not be looking for a wife, but you should be looking for a mother for Kadriye. She needs a mother, my son. Please at least meet Didenur Hanım for Kadriye's sake," Jamila insisted.

Looking at Kadriye rocking a doll in her arms, Ziya knew his mother was right.

"All right, Anne," said Ziya, "but I only agree to meet her."

Jamila was elated. She was sure Ziya would feel the same as she did when he met Didenur Hanım.

The next day Jamila went to the tekke to consult Husnu Baba. She opened the subject of a meeting between Ziya and Didenur Hanım, and Husnu Baba approved wholeheartedly. He suggested that they meet in his study at the tekke before the Friday afternoon talk.

On her way home, Jamila stopped by to see Rabia. Jamila told her about her discussions with Ziya and Husnu Baba. Then she asked Rabia if she would visit Didenur Hanım and arrange for her to meet Ziya at the tekke on Friday. Rabia said that she would be delighted to try. She immediately sent a servant to Didenur Hanım to inform her that, if convenient, she would like to visit in the afternoon. Didenur replied that she would be pleased to receive Rabia Hanım.

Rabia was more than happy to take an active role in bringing Didenur and Ziya together. Her best friend, Jamila, had suffered greatly in the past number of years. First, she had lost her beloved parents in a cholera epidemic and then her daughter-in-law. These losses were compounded by her divorce from Kamil Efendi. Rabia was hoping that the tide would turn for Jamila...

That afternoon when Rabia arrived at Aliye Sultan's palace, she was shown into a sitting room where Didenur was playing the piano. Didenur got up from the piano and welcomed Rabia.

"I don't want to interrupt your playing," Rabia said.

"Not at all," replied Didenur. "I was just passing time at the piano until you came."

A servant knocked on the door and entered, bringing coffee and sweets. When she left, Rabia broached the purpose of her visit. She explained the circumstances of the past several years: Ziya's marriage, Nilufer's death and Kadriye's birth… She also mentioned Jamila's strong desire for a good mother for Kadriye.

"You made a very positive impression on Jamila Hanım," Rabia said. "She would very much like for you to meet her son, Ziya, at the tekke. Also, Husnu Baba has given his approval. What do you think?"

"I don't know," Didenur replied. "After the ordeal of my first marriage, I am hesitant to marry again."

"I understand," Rabia continued, "but of course every man is different. I have known Ziya Bey all his life and I can assure you that he is a virtuous and evolved person."

"I'm not sure what to say. Let me think about it for a few days," replied Didenur politely.

Rabia agreed and took her leave.

Didenur thought carefully about the idea of remarrying, particularly another widower. Although in Ottoman society it was common for both women and men to remarry after divorce or the death of their spouses, Didenur was uncertain. What if like Colonel Davud, Ziya Bey also clung to the memory of his former wife? What if he was still in love with Nilufer?

In the past several years Didenur had had many offers to marry, but she politely declined them all. She had pushed the thought of remarriage to the back of her mind, and she had even suppressed her strong desire to have children. Focusing on piano playing was much safer.

On Friday morning Didenur was still undecided, so she thought it would be a good idea to consult Aliye Sultan. After explaining the circumstances, Didenur asked Aliye Sultan what she thought.

"Didenur, I understand your concerns regarding remarriage, but you don't have to make that decision yet. You are just going to meet Ziya Bey. If you do not want to procede any further after meeting him, then that is your privilege. Since Husnu Baba is in favor of this meeting, I think you should go."

Reluctantly, Didenur agreed to meet Ziya. She sent news to Rabia Hanım that she would meet Ziya Bey in Husnu Baba's study before the talk.

In the afternoon Jamila and Ziya went to the tekke early as usual. Jamila took her familiar place near the front of the balcony upstairs while Ziya waited in the sheik's study to meet Didenur Hanım. Before long, Husnu Baba entered the room followed by Didenur. Asking them both to be seated, the sheik also sat down.

After introducing Didenur to Ziya, Husnu Baba inquired about their health and happiness in general and about Kadriye in particular. He then asked Didenur about her piano teaching and praised her for her musical accomplishment. After that, he spoke extensively with Ziya about the orphanage project, even discussing many architectural details. Husnu Baba also praised this project and said he was ready to support it in any way he could. Thanking Husnu Baba, Ziya said sincerely:

"Baba, your prayers will be the best possible support."

The time for the talk was drawing close and Husnu Baba was preparing to leave. Not wanting to make the same mistake she had made with Davud, Didenur decided to look at Ziya's eyes to try and see if he was still mourning for his former wife. Shyly lifting her head and looking towards Ziya's face, Didenur saw that Ziya was looking at her face as well. Their eyes met and held for a moment. Didenur knew that Ziya was seeing her and only her.

After exchanging good-byes, Didenur and Ziya followed Husnu Baba out of the study. Ziya went to sit with the male congregation and Didenur went upstairs to the women's balcony. Didenur wanted to pay her respects to Jamila Hanım, but it was too crowded.

Didenur's mind kept drifting off during Husnu Baba's talk. She was thinking about the meeting that had just taken place. Should she allow herself to think about remarriage if Ziya Bey showed further interest? Could she take such a risk? This was the first time she was asking herself these questions since her divorce from the colonel. Didenur's mind was confused, but her heart had begun to stir.

Downstairs Ziya's attention was also drifting away from Husnu Baba's talk. After Nilufer's death, Ziya had not looked closely at any strange woman until today. When he looked at Didenur's face, he had been looking for the light that his mother was sure Didenur had. He had not been disappointed. There was a subtle light in her face, perhaps reflecting purification of the soul through pain. Ziya felt a common bond with Didenur.

After the sheik's talk was finished, Jamila Hanım and Didenur exchanged greetings. Jamila tried to read how the meeting with Ziya had gone by the look on Didenur's face, but there was no hint. She would have to wait and ask Ziya.

On the way home Jamila questioned Ziya about his meeting with Didenur. Much to her delight, Ziya confirmed that he, too, had seen the light in Didenur's face. He said, however, that he needed a little time to think the situation over before taking any further action. He was not sure about what he should do. Jamila did not want to push Ziya, so she decided to drop the subject until he was ready to discuss it further.

Chapter 10

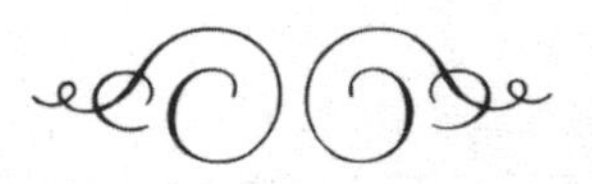

Three days after meeting Didenur in Husnu Baba's study, Ziya came into the nursery while Jamila was playing with Kadriye.

"Anne," he said, "for the past several days I have been trying to sort out my life. I've been asking myself whether I'm really ready to move beyond Nilufer's death or not. If not, it would be a cruel thing, indeed, to invite Didenur Hanım into my life. I've searched my soul to the best of my ability and I have asked for guidance from God. Hopefully I have come to the right decision."

"And what is that decision?" Jamila asked expectantly.

"I have decided to ask for Didenur Hanım's hand in marriage," replied Ziya. "Anneciğim, do you think she will accept?"

"Oh, Ziya, I truly believe you have made the right decision. We can only hope that Didenur will make the right decision as well," Jamila said.

The next day Jamila went to see Rabia. She told her about Ziya's decision and asked Rabia if she would visit Didenur Hanım and learn whether she was receptive to a marriage proposal or not. Rabia said she would be happy to.

That afternoon Rabia paid a call on Didenur. After exchanging polite courtesies, Rabia said:

"Didenur Hanım, Ziya Bey's mother has informed me that he responded positively to your meeting last Friday at the tekke. I hope Ziya Bey made a favorable impression on you, as well."

"It was only a first impression, of course," Didenur replied, "but it was a good impression."

"And does that mean you would entertain an offer of marriage from him?" Rabia asked.

"I'm not sure if I am ready to make that decision yet. To be honest, after my first unsuccessful marriage, I have difficulty trusting my own judgment again," replied Didenur.

Trying to be helpful, Rabia suggested, "Perhaps you should make the *istihare* prayer. What do you think?"

"Yes, I hadn't thought of that," replied Didenur. "Maybe the *istihare* prayer could give me clear guidance."

Happy that Didenur Hanım was at least open to considering a marriage proposal, Rabia asked for permission to leave.

Didenur decided to make the special prayer Thursday night. After making the *istihare* prayer, she asked for guidance from God in regard to marrying Ziya Bey and then went to sleep.

That night Didenur dreamt that she was back in her Circassian homeland. It was a bright and sunny day. She was standing alone in a green meadow that extended toward the horizon as far as the eye could see. While picking some flowers, she saw a horse in the distance. The horse began galloping towards her. When it halted in front of her, Didenur saw a large star on the horse's forehead. "Star, is that you?" Didenur asked in amazement. It was Star! After hugging him around the neck, Didenur mounted the horse and they started off at a trot. As they picked up more and more speed, Star's feet left the ground and they began flying through the air. They went higher and higher until they landed in the middle of a large square full of people. Everyone was celebrating. The women were all wearing beautiful dresses unlike any Didenur had ever seen before. The dresses were shimmering in different colors, as if they were illuminated from within. Young men were passing out large mugs of honey sherbet, which was flowing naturally from springs in the hillsides. When Didenur looked down, she saw that she, too, was wearing one of the shimmering dresses, only hers was a little different. It looked like it was made from crystal. As she rode around the square on Star, everyone applauded and showered her with flowers.

Didenur woke up at dawn. Remembering her dream clearly, a tingle of excitement flowed through her body. The dream had been truly magical. Didenur did not know where she had gone, but it was definitely a celestial realm. The dresses were more beautiful than any she had ever seen in this world, and the fragrance of the flowers was intoxicating. And Star… Star was magnificent. It was more than clear to Didenur that her dream was auspicious.

Today was Friday, the day of Husnu Baba's talk. Didenur went to the tekke early because she wanted to relate her dream to Husnu Baba. After describing her dream, Husnu Baba confirmed what Didenur already knew in her heart:

"Didenur *kızım*," said the sheik, "your marriage to Ziya Bey is a match made in heaven."

Didenur was so excited she did not know what to do. She thanked Husnu Baba and asked permission to leave. As she was going upstairs, she ran into Rabia Hanım.

"Didenur Hanım, I've been looking for you. I wanted to ask if you made the *istihare* prayer," said Rabia.

"Yes," Didenur replied. "I just related my dream to Husnu Baba."

"And what did he say?" Rabia asked cautiously.

"He said it was a match made in heaven," Didenur responded smilingly.

"Then we can come with Ziya Bey to ask for your hand in marriage?" Rabia asked excitedly.

"Yes, I would be honored," replied Didenur. "Next Thursday evening would be an appropriate time."

After parting from Didenur Hanım, Rabia rushed to give Jamila and Ziya the good news.

The next week seemed to crawl by for Ziya. He had proceeded cautiously about approaching remarriage after Nilufer's death. But once he had made up his mind about proposing to Didenur, he was eager to act. However, he had no choice but to wait for Thursday evening.

Jamila wanted Didenur Hanım to see Kadriye before Thursday evening, so she invited her for tea on Monday afternoon. When Didenur arrived, Jamila took her to the nursery where Kadriye was playing with her dadı.

Didenur intently watched Kadriye playing. Before long, Kadriye became tired and, unexpectedly, she put her head in Didenur's lap. Didenur took the little girl into her arms and held her as she fell asleep. The motherly love that Didenur had suppressed for so many years surfaced once again. At last she had found a child to call her own.

Observing Didenur's compassionate attitude towards Kadriye, Jamila smiled to herself. She had learned what she wanted to know: Didenur Hanım would be an attentive and caring mother...

Thursday evening Ziya and Jamila went to Aliye Sultan's palace. Ziya asked for Didenur's hand in marriage, and Didenur consented. At Ziya's insistence, the date for the official wedding ceremony was set for one week later; it would take place at Aliye Sultan's palace. That evening they also agreed upon the amount of mahr and living expenses that would be paid to Didenur.

On the way home Ziya remarked to Jamila:

"Anneciğim, just three weeks ago I had not even heard of Didenur Hanım. Now I am planning to marry her. Isn't life amazing?"

"Ziya," replied Jamila, "when you flow with the Universal Plan, everything becomes amazing, everything occurs with ease."

One week later Jamila, Ziya and Rabia went to Aliye Sultan's palace on Thursday afternoon.

As they approached the house, Jamila saw Kamil Efendi entering the door. He appeared to have aged considerably since Jamila had seen him last. Esma Sultan, the favorite sister of the Sultan, had died the previous year from pneumonia. When the Sultan recently appointed a new head physician, Kamil had been overlooked again. No longer able to entertain any hope for promotion, Kamil was a broken man.

When Jamila and Rabia entered the harem, they were greeted by Didenur, Aliye Sultan and Servetseza. Just as these women had shared Didenur's sorrow and troubled times, now they would share the joy of this occasion. The husbands of Aliye Sultan and Servetseza would act as witnesses to the marriage.

After a simple ceremony, the wedding dinner began. The men and women dined separately at elegant dining tables. Didenur looked striking in an ice-blue silk organza gown Aliye Sultan had given her as a gift. After dinner Jamila presented her with a diamond and sapphire necklace; a diamond ring had been sent previously.

At the insistence of Aliye Sultan, Didenur played several pieces on the piano. At the end of the recital, Servetseza remarked:

"Ziya Bey is very fortunate, indeed. He is not only getting an excellent wife, but an extraordinary pianist as well."

All the women smiled. "You can rest assured that all of Didenur Hanım's talents will be well appreciated," replied Jamila.

"Didenur and Servetseza are like sisters to me," commented Aliye Sultan. "We grew up together in the palace and I have many fond memories from those days. I've also been fortunate to have the constant companionship of Didenur during the last four years. I have to admit that I'm going to miss her dearly."

"My Sultan, you have provided a safe haven for me in my time of greatest need. I'll be eternally grateful to you," replied Didenur.

After the women finished drinking their coffee, Aliye Sultan called in some dancers and musicians to entertain her guests. It was a memorable evening for everyone.

When the entertainment ended, Jamila and the other guests asked for permission to leave. Aliye Sultan reluctantly granted it. Carriages were waiting outside to take everyone home.

When Didenur entered her new home in Beylerbeyi, a surprise was waiting for her in the harem reception hall. Didenur was thrilled to see a new Steinway piano.

"I keep hearing about your musical talent. Aren't you going to play for me?" Ziya asked Didenur.

"As you wish," Didenur replied. She sat down at the piano and began to play. But the piano was no longer a medium for her sorrow and longing. Tonight her music reflected the new hope in her heart.

"Everyone is right; your music is truly exquisite," Ziya said, thinking that Didenur's music must be an expression of her finely tuned soul.

After Ziya and Didenur said goodnight to Jamila, they retired to their own suite. Didenur felt a little tense. She could not help but remember the disappointment and rejection she had felt on the first night of her marriage with Davud.

Ziya sensed Didenur's apprehension. Taking her into his arms, he looked into her eyes and said:

"Didenur, you are my wife now and you are the sole focus of my manly love. There is no one else standing between us. There is only a nascent love that will grow and bloom as long as we carefully cultivate it."

Intuitively, Didenur trusted Ziya…

Her trust was not misplaced. Ziya took the lead in cultivating their love. He was a gentle and attentive lover, a devoted and responsible husband, and a sincere and caring friend and partner. Didenur responded in kind. In Ziya she had found a man she could truly love, trust and respect. She did her best to show her appreciation.

Jamila was all that the colonel's mother had not been. She was kind, courteous, supportive and appreciative. She whole-heartedly accepted Didenur as her daughter, and she frequently praised Didenur for her relationship with Kadriye.

Didenur was a naturally compassionate mother, but Kadriye's having lost her mother at birth made Didenur even more sensitive to the little girl's needs. She was determined to do her best for Kadriye.

In time Didenur's past reservations about conceiving a child disappeared. She felt safe and secure in Ziya's love and now, more than ever, she wanted to have children. It did not take long for her wish to be fulfilled. A year after they married, Didenur gave birth to twins.

With a baby in each arm and Kadriye on her lap, Didenur's happiness was unbounded. She remembered the words of the stranger who had given her hot stew while she was in captivity: "Don't be frightened little one. Many have made this journey before you. If God wills, you will have a life better than you could ever dream of…" He was right. Didenur could not have imagined this bliss – a devoted husband, a supportive mother-in-law, sincere and caring friends, three healthy children and a respectable and comfortable position among the Ottoman elite. Didenur had had to endure some very difficult and painful trials, but this moment made it all worthwhile…

Jamila was also elated by the birth of the twins. On the one hand, she felt it would be good for Kadriye to have a brother and sister and, on the other hand, she knew how much Didenur and Ziya wanted children. However, Jamila was not yet able to devote a great deal of time to the new-borns because she was preoccupied with preparations for the opening of the new orphanage.

Located on a lot of land in Uskudar which Jamila had inherited from her parents, the orphanage was situated on a hill overlooking the Bosphorus. Ziya had overseen construction of the building, which had begun shortly after his marriage to Didenur. The wooden building consisted of a large kitchen and hamam on the ground floor, two large reception rooms on the second floor, and study rooms surrounded by four large dormitory rooms on the second and third floors.

The construction of the orphanage was complete. After Jamila put the final touches on the furnishings, she went to the tekke to invite Husnu Baba to make a prayer at the opening ceremonies. Husnu Baba gladly accepted the invitation. While she had the sheik's attention, Jamila decided to also ask him about something that had been on her mind for a long time:

"Husnu Baba, when Kamil asked for my hand in marriage, my mother made the *istihare* prayer to see if that marriage would be good for me. She saw me sitting in a room playing with a doll on the seventh floor of a building. In the dream she asked her god-mother, Hayriye Ana, what I was doing there. Hayriye Ana replied that although my mother was not aware of it, I would rise very high in this life.

"My parents wanted to ask you to interpret this dream, but you were in Mecca at the time so it was not possible. Thinking that the dream was auspicious, we proceeded with the marriage. As you know, Kamil Bey and I have divorced now. So I'm wondering if perhaps the dream wasn't a good omen after all," Jamila said.

"Jamila *kızım*," replied Husnu Baba, "haven't you risen high in this life? You have risen above the domination of your own needs and desires and your life is now focused on fulfilling the needs of others. It is true that you have lost your husband in the process, but that is because Kamil Efendi is still focused primarily on his own needs. You no longer share the same purpose in life, so you no longer attract each other. Each human being's spiritual journey is unique. At times, you may be synchronized with another person, but at other times you may not be.

"On the other hand, we are tested by means of those closest to us. We become vehicles for the spiritual development of each other, sometimes positively and sometimes negatively. Your relationship with Kamil Efendi has been a trial and a test for you, Jamila *kızım*, but I would say that you have passed this test admirably."

"Thank you, Husnu Baba," replied Jamila. "I never looked at it that way."

On the day of the opening ceremonies Ziya and Jamila left for the orphanage early in the morning to make sure all the preparations were complete. On the way Ziya said:

"Anneciğim, Didenur and I feel we have accomplished a lot with three children, but you have fifty children. Your success is difficult to match."

Jamila smiled and asked: "Ziya, do you want to know the secret to this success?"

"Of course, you have my full attention," Ziya responded.

"It's all about our world view, my son. When we are children, our world is limited to our own needs and happiness. At that stage in life, we basically only know how to receive. When we grow older, our world expands to include the needs and happiness of others, our families in particular. At this stage we both give and expect to receive. But there is even a broader world beyond that, Ziya, which many people never envision. It is all about loving other creatures for the sake of the Creator, about caring for others with no expectations of anything in return. This stage of life is all about giving. But the interesting point here is that the more you give, the more you receive back from the Universe. You get things you could never have thought of asking for. Believe me, my son, I never asked for fifty chidren. I just wanted to help a few orphans; I just took the first step. Everything else took care of itself."

"I know exactly what you mean, Anneciğim," said Ziya. "From the very beginning I have watched this orphanage project unfold like a ball of yarn unraveling. I'm curious as to where things will go from here."

"Actually, I've already been thinking about that," Jamila said smilingly with a twinkle in her eye. "Since this orphanage is for boys, shouldn't we build one for girls as well?"

Ziya returned his mother's smile with open admiration and love in his eyes…

The carriage pulled up to the orphanage. Jamila and Ziya got down and went inside. There was an atmosphere of immense excitement everywhere. On the previous day fifty orphan boys had been brought from various places in Istanbul to reside together at the orphanage. They had spent their first night at their new home under the care of a supervisor and five assistants. The boys had gotten up early and put on their new clothes in anticipation of today's celebration. After the opening ceremonies, the children would all be given gifts carefully prepared by the women from the waqf. A small ferris wheel and other rides had been set up on the orphanage grounds to entertain the boys.

The smell of roast lamb and halwa wafted in the air as the door to the kitchen opened and closed. Jamila went to the small office on the first floor to wait for Husnu Baba while Ziya made a last-minute inspection of the premises. Looking out the window which overlooked the Straits, Jamila felt an intense feeling of serenity and inner peace.

Before long, Husnu Baba arrived at the orphanage. His ever-present smile seemed to be even broader today.

"Jamila *kızım*," he said, "you have found the golden key to happiness: helping others. When Ziya was growing up, you were able to help shape the future of one child. Now your opportunity has increased fifty-fold. Now you are helping to shape the future of fifty children. May God bless you and increase your success."

Jamila smiled and said softly, "You're right, Husnu Baba, from one perspective I am helping to shape the future of fifty children. But from another perspective I am opening up fifty new channels of love…"